Our first & Last

BECCA SEYMOUR

──── RAINBOW TREE PUBLISHING ────

ALSO BY BECCA SEYMOUR

COMING HOME COLLECTION

Realigned

Amalgamated

TRUE-BLUE SERIES

Let Me Show You (#1) | I've Got You (#2) | Becoming Us
(#3) | Thinking It Over (#4)| Always For You (#5) | It's
Not You (#6) | Our First & Last (#7)

OUTBACK BOYS SERIES

Stumble (#1)

Bounce (#2)

STAND-ALONE CONTEMPORARY

Not Used To Cute

URBAN FANTASY ROMANCE

Thicker Than Water

For information, contact the author:
authorbeccaseymour@gmail.com

Editing: Hot Tree Editing

Cover Designer: BookSmith Design

Publisher: Rainbow Tree Publishing

E-book ISBN: 978-1-922359-83-4

Paperback ISBN: 978-1-922359-85-8

"Live authentically. Live your truth."

- Neale Donald Walsch

CHAPTER ONE

IAN

IT DIDN'T MATTER HOW OFTEN HE BENT OVER, HOW regular or familiar the movement, tearing my gaze away proved impossible. He filled out the jeans to perfection. Every time I saw the man—regardless of how many weeks passed between my visits—I never seemed to get my fill.

The problem? I was setting myself up for a heart attack. The man was unattainable. Full stop. End of story.

Straight men didn't tend to fall for their gay friends. Sure, I'd heard of more than one exception, but that didn't seem likely in this instance. Even though the man setting up one of the street stores for the start of tomorrow's Pride festival happily waved a rainbow flag in support of his brother and his friends—me included—Frankie Harrison was 100 percent straight.

Him being a dad and me hearing about a couple of his past conquests pretty much confirmed that. While he'd never come out and declared his sexuality, in all my years, I'd never known a straight person—male or female—to have a need to. It was one of those luxuries, I supposed, of being straight—never having to clarify they were into people of the opposite sex.

Not that I'd want my life any other way, though.

While I'd been a relatively late bloomer and hadn't come out until I was in my third year at college, since that moment of liberation, I'd lived happily as an out and proud man. Perhaps the fact I was studying to be a nurse meant that my classmates weren't overly surprised, which weirdly frustrated me that the stereotype about male nurses existed. It shouldn't matter that I was absolutely gay and a nurse. I knew plenty of straight male nurses.

"You about done here?"

Jasper's voice pulled me away from my buzzing brain, thinking about Frankie's ass and straight nurses, with a jolt. I looked across at my friend and bobbed my head. "Will be in five. What's next?"

"Frankie could do with a hand setting up the lucky dip store."

Controlling the blush that threatened to steal across my face, I smiled. "Sure thing."

"Stop slacking," Frankie hollered, no doubt having heard his name.

I glanced in his direction. My smile immediately softened when we made eye contact. The man turned my insides to mush. It was incredible how, for the past two years, I'd managed to function around him.

That was the thing with Frankie, though. He was casual and kindness personified. From our first meeting all that time ago, I'd been at ease with him. More than once, I'd told him he could charm the pants off a snake. Not once did he deny it. The man had skills for sure.

The difficulty was, I desperately wanted him to practice those skills on me.

"You'd know all about that," I sassed. "All the years of bumming around the world perfected your talent. How many stalls is that you've set up now, in what —" I looked at my nonexistent watch. "—two hours?"

"Hush now, but here, take this." He shoved his hand in his pocket, only to remove it and flip me off.

I snorted a laugh. "That's not one of the many pearls of wisdom you've shared with Tyler, right?" I quirked my brow at him, knowing full well he was a great dad.

Frankie chuckled while I grinned as I punched in the last staple. "As if. I swore once, *once*, and the kid said that one slip-up of a word to every single person he met for a whole two weeks. No chance of that happening again."

I headed over to him, remembering all too well when Tyler gave me a hug about a year back, telling me he missed me like a motherfucker. Even now, I had no clue how I kept a straight face as I hugged him back, saying I'd missed him more.

"Where do you want me?" The words were out, and I clamped on the inside of my cheeks with my back teeth. Obviously, I would have seriously liked a range of answers from him, ones flirty but real. The Frankie I crushed so hard over rarely missed an opportunity for innuendo. The lack of "real" connected to such offers always hit hard.

"Anywhere that won't give you grass stains."

I shook my head, snorting despite the rush of heat unfurling in my stomach. "You didn't strike me as a man worried about a bit of mess. There's a lot to be said about stains." Once again, I slammed my mouth shut. He did this to me every single time. I couldn't not flirt with the man. It was dangerous and, I was sure, unhealthy considering my fixation on him. But hell if I didn't enjoy it. Frankie 100 percent brought this flirty, fun side out of me.

The sensation was addictive. Just like he was.

Frankie laughed loudly, his eyes not straying from mine. Amusement danced in their depths. What I wouldn't give for one day there to be something more looking from his pretty eyes. "Uh-oh. Fredrick's coming over." The wide eyes he shot my way had me snorting in amusement. "Best look like we're busy."

"We are super busy," I insisted with a wink as I gathered the signage that needed to be put up. As I did so, I gave a quick head bob to Fredrick, who fortunately was called over by someone else. "Close call."

"Tell me about it. You're lucky you still don't live here yet. The guy's a tyrant."

"He's not that bad."

Frankie's brows shot high as he helped me with the sign by standing wonderfully close, his arm brushing my chest as he held the material in place so I could staple it. The area burned at the contact but in the best of ways. Not like a urine infection or anything. More like the gentle heat of a hot stone massage. "I don't know what Ted was thinking," I said after swallowing hard and keeping my shaky voice at bay.

"I don't think he had much choice in who was on the Pride committee from the two other towns outside of Kirkby. But I wouldn't worry too much about Ted. As if anyone is going to steamroll his baby."

It was true. Ted, a local bar owner, had spearheaded the whole LGBTIA+ event. And being a part of it, even though one of my roles tomorrow made me a little nervous, was great. Me spending the whole weekend with my good friends at my side, Frankie being high on the list, was worth the cramp forming in my thumb from all the damn stapling.

CHAPTER TWO

FRANKIE

SURROUNDED BY LAUGHTER IN TED AND JASON'S BAR, I eased back in the chair with a smile. The day had been busy finalizing everything for tomorrow's festival. There'd been a whole team working on the preparations the past few days, but today was full-on.

The hard work would be totally worth it, though.

Having a Pride festival—complete with a mini-parade and a bunch of activities and stalls—in a small town like Kirkby still boggled my mind. I supposed it said a lot about Ted. He'd made a decision last year that with the growing LGBTQI+ community, not only in Kirkby but the two other surrounding towns, we could finally handle the event. And looking around the packed bar filled with grinning faces, I knew the man was right.

"Ian," I called over to him. He stood with a drink in hand while angling around, clearly searching.

His gaze caught mine, and his lips curved high. Immediately he made his way over, and I shuffled over on the small booth bench seat to make room for him. It would be a tight fit, considering the man's bulk, but there was no hardship with having him close to my side.

I was a glutton for punishment. Not only did I enjoy Ian's company more than was appropriate for the friendship we had, but I craved physical contact with him. I wasn't quite sure how much longer I could last without making a move.

"Thanks." He sat by my side, his defined arms pressing against mine. My whole body seemed to sigh at the contact. "I've never seen this place so busy. How'd you manage to score a seat?"

"I have my ways." I waggled my brows, and he smiled, a light pink coloring his cheeks.

"A room filled with men and women glitzed up in a rainbow of colors; I can only imagine just how easy that was." He glanced around the room as he spoke, but I only had eyes for him and how his Adam's apple bobbed when he swallowed his beer.

Glutton. For. Punishment.

It was times like these, with Ian wedged against me and me being incredibly comfortable in his company, I begrudged my self-inflicted rules since moving.

There was my boy, Ty, to think about. He was at the top of the list, truth be told. Having had such a rough start in life, my son needed stability, so me hooking up with anyone, let alone starting up something with Ian when he didn't live locally, wasn't on the agenda.

There was no doubt when Ian's situation changed, though, and he finally moved locally, I'd make my interest clear. A brand-new agenda would be assigned for sure. The man was incredible and such a good guy. I'd be a fool to not try.

"Where's Tyler?"

It was no wonder I liked him so much. He adored my son, a sure way to wedge himself in my heart. "Jenna's looking after him. I need to head out soon to pick him up and get him home to bed. I imagine he's played out with her boys."

"I'm sure he's loved every moment."

"I have no doubt. He's excited for tomorrow."

"Jasper said something about him dressing up."

I laughed, thinking about my boy and the costume he was determined to wear.

"What?"

I angled to look at Ian when he spoke, enjoying how his gaze roamed mine and landed on my mouth. That sweet blush was there too, and not for the first time I suspected he liked me a little more than as a friend too. I had everything crossed that he'd get a call soon with a job offer. My world was more than big enough to have him in it—and for the long haul, I hoped. "I think maybe it should be a surprise if Jasper hasn't already told you."

Ian quirked his brow. "Hell no. Tell me what that cute kid of yours is wearing."

Unable to resist and wanting to see his reaction, I said, "You. He wants to be just like you so is going as a nurse."

Ian's eyes widened before softening. "Really?" His voice dropped, tenderness evident in that one word.

"The kid's got good taste. You know he thinks you're a superhero." My cock twitched as Ian's blush renewed, this time fiercer and so much more adorable.

"Well," he said, rubbing at the back of his neck, "I think he's the one who's a hero."

Ian was going to destroy me. My fingers twitched, begging to reach out and haul him close. And he was right. Ty was a hero. He was the most resilient kid I knew. Bouncing back from his mom's death the way he had was incredible. He'd survived her loss, beat back the nightmares, and accepted fully that I was his dad and I wasn't going anywhere.

I swallowed back my emotion for my extraordinary boy and the amazing man at my side. "I suppose I should add he's jumped all over every rainbow and LGBTQ thing going. He's going full-on sparkly rainbow unicorn nurse." Amusement mixed with my pride as I spoke.

Ian's laughter rolled over me. "I can't wait to see him. If he's not ready by the time I have to leave to head out tomorrow, make sure you find me as soon as possible."

"He'll be awake and ready. The kid's so excited. I fear dress-up may be the next big thing for Ty. I'm half expecting him to be one of those kids who rock up at pre-k wearing a new costume every day."

"It makes birthday and Christmas gifts easier."

I snorted. "That it does."

A couple of chairs opposite our bench seat opened up but were quickly occupied by a cute guy wearing blue eyeshadow and a larger, older man wearing a three-piece suit.

"Hey," I greeted them, eyeing the suit. "Looking sharp, but aren't you melting in that?" It had been a warm day, and with the thickness of the crowd in the bar, the heat was a little oppressive.

The suit guy smiled at me and shook his head. "I'm good. I'm used to it."

I didn't recognize either man as locals, but that meant nothing. It wasn't like I was familiar with every person across the community. It also wasn't like I got out very often.

"You both from around here?" the cute one wearing eyeshadow asked, staring at Ian, clearly hungry for a taste.

I refrained from edging closer and claiming him as my own. Being all possessive when I had no right to be would be a shitty move. And for all I knew, Ian might be interested. The thought clenched around my heart, which was not liking the possibility one bit. Maybe I should at least have the conversation with the man, let him know what was going on in my head and my heart, but being a selfish fucker was a thing of my past. Or at least, I was trying my hardest for it to be.

When I'd left home at eighteen for college and after that headed out immediately to travel the world— chasing the high of snowboarding—I didn't think too much about my family, who I'd left behind. Instead, I'd been living it up, working my way through resorts and between the legs of anyone who I'd found attractive.

It wasn't until I was at college that I embraced the real me. Experimentation became my mission until that became my lifestyle of fucking and partying. The thing was, I had no regrets about how I'd lived, how and who I spent time with and buried inside. Unequivocally, I'd made my own rules, label-free and living how I wanted.

Now, with my responsibilities, I recognized a couple of things. The first being, I missed out on a lot of time with my family. At times I regretted doing so, but living with guilt wasn't my MO. The second thing I recognized since being a dad was Ty needed to be at the center of every decision I made. And while I wanted someone in my life and my hopes were set on Ian, I had to at least try to be smart and not think with my dick.

When Ian didn't answer, I cast him a quick glance. I recognized and didn't like the discomfort settled on his face. "I am, but a recent transplant. My friend here, not yet, but hopefully that'll change soon."

Ian's eyes connected with mine and lit up at my words, a smile pushing the brightness into them that I was used to.

"Cool. We have friends in Chester Fields. We can't believe we've never driven these few miles further out and been to Kirkby before. It's a nice place." The smaller guy wore a friendly smile, his gaze now on me.

"The whole area is great. Definitely worth spending some time here."

"Is that an offer?" he asked with a flirty smile, his gaze dancing between Ian and me. "We're more than happy to share a big bed for four."

Ian choked on the mouthful of beer, and I turned to him, concerned. "You okay?" I placed my hand on his back, ready to start smacking at it should I need to.

"Yes," he spluttered. "Just went down the wrong way."

Once he was able to breathe, I turned my attention back to the cute guy, casting a not-so-subtle glance at the suit-wearing man too. Watching me, he appeared super relaxed. Maybe in another life, I would have taken them up on the offer, but being my responsible self meant my answer was a reluctant no, and sharing Ian with anyone was a hard fucking no.

"Not for me, thanks. I have to head home soon." I worked hard at keeping my muscles relaxed and casual when I glanced at Ian. Should he be interested in spending time with the two men, which he had every right to, I was sure a small part of my heart would fracture.

"Thanks for the offer, but Frankie's my ride."

"Oh, so you're not together?" the guy wearing eyeshadow asked.

Ian shook his head but remained silent. Discomfort rolled off him, and I racked my brains as to why. I looked back at the two men. They seemed friendly enough, and neither seemed offended by our brush-off. It had been a while— I paused at that thought. Actually, I couldn't remember the last time Ian mentioned hooking up with anyone. Jasper, his best friend, hadn't said anything either.

But what I did know was he'd had a couple of incidents when he'd been hit on to the point of discomfort. It seemed there were assholes in this world who saw a fit, athletic man and thought that meant they could be pushy to the point of intimidation. Those stories had pissed me off. Ian was a gentle guy. From my understanding, he could handle himself at work, being assertive and very much in control as ER nurses needed to be. But strip away his uniform, and he was a big, fluffy marshmallow. One I'd happily dote on and care for given a chance.

"Ian's being coy. Not together doesn't mean to say he's not mine." I reached out and gently squeezed the back of his neck. His skin was warm, soft, and perfect under my touch.

The suit grinned. "Perhaps your friend here needs reminding that he's yours more often if he's uncertain."

"Perhaps you're right," I answered immediately. "And on that note, we really should get out of here." My attention turned to Ian. Red stole across his cheeks, and his eyes were wide. "Do you want to finish your beer or are you ready?"

Once again, my focus moved to his bobbing Adam's apple. This time it wasn't swallowing beer that was the cause.

"I'm good to go now."

I sent him a warm smile. "Come on then." I looked at the two guys. "Have a good night. I hope you find what you're looking for."

"I'm sure we will," the younger guy answered. "Have fun."

We left the booth, tension thrumming through me. Being alone in the car together wasn't a great idea, not as the need to make good on my words rode me. Spotting my brother and Jasper, I headed in their direction, making sure Ian remained close. "Hey," I greeted. "I'm heading off. You guys good to give Ian a lift back?" I felt shitty for saying so, considering what I'd said moments ago, but in truth, Ian had arrived with Jasper and Austin.

When I glanced at my brother, his gaze was intent, a little too much so. There was little doubt I was acting strangely. While I had to pick up Ty, he'd be asleep in five minutes. There was no way I'd be able to concentrate with Ian by my side on the journey home, not with the renewed buzzing of want flooding my system.

"Of course," Jasper answered, not seeming at all suspicious, but the happy glow of alcohol was unmistakable.

"Have a good night, and I'll see you guys in the morning." I turned away from them, pausing when I looked at Ian. His gaze was awash with an emotion I didn't want to think about. But it was no good. I'd hurt him. I exhaled slowly and offered him a wide smile that was fake as fuck. "Get ready for all the cuteness of Ty you're going to see tomorrow." God, I was a manipulative bastard, throwing my son at him to erase the hurt from his eyes.

"I can't wait."

I reached out and hugged him, unable to resist, and aware a small hug was how we usually said hello and goodbye. Maybe I held on a little too long and squeezed a little too possessively, but when he didn't seem eager to let me go, I sighed into the touch before hightailing it out of there.

CHAPTER THREE

IAN

DAUNTED, I STARED AT THE BOOTH. YESTERDAY I'D BEEN hesitantly excited, thinking it would all be a bit of fun, but now, in the thick of the bustling crowd, I wondered what on earth I'd gotten myself into.

It would be an interesting way to spend my time for sure. I shook off my nerves. The combination of LGBTQIA+ charities and being involved in Kirkby's first Pride festival was a good thing.

I exhaled and tried to get into the spirit of the event before crossing the crowd of people to the small booth. On the chalkboard was my name sketched out and surrounded with kisses.

I narrowed my eyes at the sign, certain this was the handiwork of Ted; it had not looked like this yesterday.

Snorting, I skirted around the side and stepped to the back. The stall wasn't closed off, so there was no semblance of privacy. A quick glance around the area, and I eyed the price chart I was meant to hang from the nail hammered in on the front. Five bucks for a kiss.

I shook my head.

I'd tried to convince Ted to make the smart move and let me offer shoulder massages for fifteen bucks a pop, but he'd made it clear in the ten minutes for a shoulder massage, I could make a lot more cash by merely puckering up. *Fun*, I reminded myself.

I cracked my neck, angling it side to side, for a moment wishing I wasn't single and one of the committee member's best friends. I'd sworn half-heartedly that this was going against some sort of bro code, only to be met with eye rolls and a promise to take me out clubbing next time Jasper and Austin headed out for a visit.

Okay, perhaps I didn't battle too hard.

Daphne, someone who I'd met yesterday setting up today's festivities, hadn't been exactly helpful either with my growing nerves. She was in the same boat as me. Single and had overly helpful friends. But she'd taken her hour's stint, puckering up to a line of women earlier in the day, without complaint. She'd also taken great delight in shaking her bucket of cash.

Not that I was precisely competitive, but who was I kidding? She'd riled me up just a little, and I wanted to make a shit ton of cash if I could. But that would mean getting a line going.

It wasn't like I was a prude. And in the past, I'd gotten about a fair bit. According to my brother Matty, a little too much, but he was just a jealous dick who'd been married at twenty and had a bunch of kids, meaning his fun was massively different from my own. He didn't know that over the past eighteen months or so, the guys I'd slept with could be counted on one hand. Okay, just two fingers. But honestly, I hadn't been feeling it. My heart investing in Frankie meant casual sex wasn't as fun anymore.

The last thing I wanted was to let anyone down, though. Hence me actually arriving at the festival.

Was it worth the three-hour drive? I reluctantly admitted it was, especially as the smiling faces of the three local communities coming together to celebrate the LGBTQIA+ community was pretty special.

Despite not living here, I'd become a familiar face for the past couple of years and had built a network of good friends.

It still surprised me that it had happened in this cutesy town, but I wasn't knocking it. If the opportunity arose and a nursing position became vacant, I'd be all over it.

While I'd changed jobs a year back to a quieter hospital, one with a little less stress and a lot less overtime, Kirkby called to me. And my friends here all knew it, so kept their eyes and ears open for the slightest whisper of a position coming up.

I just had to keep hoping that it would happen one day soon.

It was crazy hot in the open air, the heat feeling more like summer than early spring. It seemed like we were just having a wild few days of unseasonal temperatures, making everyone a little hot under the collar—me especially, considering my reluctance to be manning the kissing booth.

Could I have gotten out of it if I really wanted to? I sighed at the thought, knowing, of course, the answer was yes. No one, especially not Jasper, would ever force me to participate. But it didn't make me feel less awkward.

The crowds were thickening as the day headed to late afternoon, but the lateness didn't deter the sun. The sooner I started, the sooner I could get out of here.

I grabbed a mint from my pocket, then quickly checked my wallet. There was a couple of hundred bucks tucked away as a last-minute contingency. I wasn't expecting to need it though. A few guys I'd already spotted had told me they'd be sure to check out my booth at my allotted time. While my ego enjoyed the boost, it didn't deter my discomfort. But, I reminded myself, I was in control of this situation.

The charity booth wasn't about guys forcing themselves on me, trying to steal kisses. This was me accepting a brief peck on the lips and making money for charity.

An innocent kiss when I was in control was fine. I could handle it. Though Fredrick, one of the people on the committee, a bizarre man who lived in Chester Falls two towns over, had made it clear that I couldn't be putting on free porn and offer a show, so absolutely no tongues were to be involved, apparently. I'd snorted, more than okay with that when he'd told me, only to realize he was deadly serious.

I knew this was a family-friendly event, and God only knew what he was expecting from me. Obviously, he didn't know I was all but celibate these days. But still, I expected he'd taken one glance at me and made a common assumption. There was no point in being annoyed by it. I looked after myself, spent time in the gym in my downtime—more for my mental health than any other reason. The truth was, he and anyone else could make all the assumptions they wanted. Long ago, I'd made peace with who I was.

And I wasn't changing for anyone.

I opened the curtain and peered out to the masses— the masses consisting of Ted and Jason, the local bar owners. I laughed and pulled out the small bowl of breath mints Daphne had left on the small table behind the stall—I assumed specifically for customers.

"No tongues, and breath mints appreciated." I followed up with a deep laugh. "Who's first?"

Jason stepped forward. "Apparently, we're here to be supportive and get a crowd going. I can just give you the money?" His desire for me to accept the cash and let him leave was loud and clear, but no way would I cheat—I ignored the existence of the money burning a hole in my wallet—not with Fredrick probably hiding away with binoculars or something.

I clutched my chest. "Jason, Jason, Jason, you saying you don't want to lay one on me?" I gasped in over-the-top shock, completely ignoring his quirked brow and expression that suggested he'd lay something on me if I didn't hurry the hell up. "You offend me." I threw him a wink, knowing perfectly well he was a happily married man and had zero interest in anything I was offering. Meanwhile, his husband, Ted, stood with a wide grin on his face.

Jason scrunched his nose a little. "Ian, you're like a kid brother or something." He gave a whole-body shudder.

I laughed harder, more than aware we were super close in age for a start and that he really was being coerced into participating. "Just get your lips over here and give me five bucks."

He did so reluctantly, and I planted my lips against his. It was the briefest of pecks, much to both of our relief. I thanked him for being a good sport.

"Here." He shoved a five-dollar bill in the bucket and stepped back, giving a pointed look at his husband. "Your turn." He all but pushed Ted my way.

"Oh, handsome, I can get there myself. No need to push me on the buff studmuffin." Ted smirked at Jason, stage-whispering, "My tongue belongs to only you, my love. Never fear." Jason simply rolled his eyes, amusing me even more and actually doing an excellent job at relaxing my taut muscles. "Pucker up, sweetheart," Ted said with a flutter of his eyelashes.

I grinned, grabbed his face, and placed a barely there kiss on his mouth. It was closed-mouthed, and our lips hardly touched, but I added extra smooching sound effects for the occasion.

When I pulled back, he feigned a swoon. "Everyone is going to be so damn jealous. Wait till I tell them Ian Haughton is an eleven." He threw me a wink and shoved a ten-dollar bill in the bucket.

"You're my hero," I said to him. "Catch you later."

"Will do." He waved at me, tugged Jason's arm, and headed away.

Countless kisses later, one from a guy who offered me a number, despite clearly being with someone, and another who'd tried to talk me into letting him kiss another part of my anatomy, I was eager for my hour to end. Most had donated more than the five-dollar fee, which was great, and my money bucket was looking impressively full, but who knew kissing, even innocently, could be such a drain.

I sent a quick text to Jasper in a lull, reminding him that he owed me a beer, and lots of it, after this, and a bottle of mouthwash.

My phone buzzed with a reply just as I popped another mint into my mouth.

Jasper: You're loving it, diva.

I snorted. **Me: Diva my ass. Spin it. I want the beers waiting in the back of my car. I left it open.**

Jasper: Ha. You wish. Anything interesting?

I rolled my eyes. Jasper knew my conquests had been few and far between. It was sweet that he was worried about me. I blamed my lack of interest on being busy at work, but when I'd changed jobs and my love life hadn't improved, his concern had doubled. Sharing with him the details of my crush was a no-go. With Frankie being his in-law, it was all too close for comfort. The last thing I wanted was to put him in a tricky spot.

Me: Meh! Need mouthwash. Stat.

Jasper: Ha. That bad?

Me: Snort. Times a hundred.

Admittedly, I was exaggerating. While I was tired and definitely over being here, it had actually been quite fun. There were lots of new faces. I had no clue if they were from here or from one of the surrounding towns, or maybe they'd even traveled from out of the area. Either way, there was an impressive crowd, and it was good to see Ted's brainchild so successful.

I stuffed my phone in my pocket with a smile as I looked out into the busy festival. My muscles became taut when I spotted a familiar face that didn't fit this setting. Leroy. Questions about why he was here buzzed in my brain. I hoped to hell he kept on walking.

He didn't.

Holding back my groan, I remained stoic when his eyes lit up and he all but danced his boney ass over to me.

Shit.

"My oh my, if it isn't the man with the heavenly muscles." He glanced to the side, his eyes widening even more when he took in the signs. "You know I've been waiting for the chance to get my mouth on you."

I barely contained my shudder. This guy was a pain in the butt; not the good kind. I'd first met him when I'd tagged along to one of Jasper's friends' bachelor parties. It was in the city a while back. He'd tried it on then, but he wasn't my type—he wasn't Frankie. Plus, he was a creep. Since then, he'd struggled to take no for an answer, despite the fact we lived nowhere near each other. But still, he hounded me on social media and by text—a mistake I'd wished I could take back when the group of us on the night out exchanged numbers. The guy was as persistent as a mosquito. And just as irritating. If I could have, I would have swatted him away a long time ago.

He'd actually been refreshingly quiet over the past few weeks. I'd hoped that meant he'd met someone. Maybe he had, and it had since gone pear-shaped. But him being here now boggled my brain completely. He lived miles away and wasn't friends with Jasper, so I had no idea how he'd heard about this small-town event.

"You know, I only have a fifty-dollar bill, and I'm more than willing to donate all of that if I get my money's worth."

Honest to God vomit swirled in my gut. The epitome of sleaze vibe wasn't helped by his too-close-together eyes or the cigarette stench that came off him.

Panicked and far too polite for my own damn good, I flicked my eyes up to the crowd.

Frantically searching for a solution, I was sure I heard a "Hallelujah" chorus when the crowd parted and my gaze landed on the only figure I recognized.

Whether it was serendipitous or a cruel joke, I had no idea. But regardless of my feelings and the sliver of hurt that had penetrated me yesterday when for the first time, I thought he felt something more for me, the man across the crowd would have my back.

Without exception or doubt, I knew that.

"Frankie," I hollered, not giving a shit that I was grasping at straws. Holding my breath, I looked on as Frankie lifted his head, searching. Finally, his eyes landed on mine, and thank Christ, he smiled. He took the steps necessary toward me. The whole time, I was aware Leroy was angling around to look at who I'd called, not looking especially happy he no longer held my attention.

"There's the man himself." With wide eyes and a fixed smile on my face, I stared hard at Frankie. I hoped he knew me well enough to recognize my need to be saved.

His gaze flickered over the stall, a smirk appearing on his face before it landed on Leroy and returned to me. "You about done?" he asked, and I could have knelt and kissed his feet.

"Actually," Leroy said, "he had room for just one more—"

"—which would be me," Frankie interjected.

"There's a line, and I was here fi—"

"Sorry." Frankie stepped close to the booth, standing eye to eye with me and a couple of inches shorter than Leroy. "You'll find I was here first."

I swallowed hard, his words taking me by surprise and making it so unbelievably difficult to remember he was not only straight, but a friend, plus my best friend's brother-in-law.

Leroy's voice turned high-pitched. "You know each other?"

I somehow stopped the eye roll trying to break free from the redundant question since I'd just called Frankie over.

"And some," Frankie answered, surprising me again. I grinned in relief and amusement.

"So, the last kiss…" Frankie tilted his head to the side, his eyes lit with humor. "Looks like that last kiss is mine."

My gaze sprang to his before it roamed his face, taking in the man before me. There was the same smile, the same eyes, the same small scar on his temple, which he'd got walking into his son's jungle gym last fall. The guy before me was one hell of a man. I cursed the heat spreading through my chest. *Straight man.* I forced the thought to the surface, knowing crushing on Frankie any more than I already did was unhealthy as hell.

"Definitely yours," I finally answered, trying to behave like a human being and form words. It didn't stop the errant thought of *Our first* from penetrating my mind.

Frankie edged closer, and his lips twitched. Pounding beats of my heart rushed through my ears, making it difficult to hear, let alone think. This was ridiculous. My reaction. My inability to keep my shit together and not swoon and drool over the guy who kept creeping into my heart.

I was aware of Leroy slightly off to the side and assumed Frankie had edged him away. Despite our location, the loud noise of the festival, the large groups wandering by, and the flash of rainbow colors filling up almost every area of the field, with my eyes fixed on Frankie, the noises and crowds blurred.

His hand moving to his wallet broke my gaze. He then smiled and angled forward, his mouth a hairsbreadth from mine.

I hadn't even realized I'd leaned so far over to get to him.

"So…."

"Hmmm?"

"The last kiss is mine, right?"

I forgot to breathe but somehow managed to bob my head.

Frankie's response was a slight quirk of his lips as he raised his palm and swept his thumb over my bottom lip. The roaring appeared once again in my ears. Our gaze connected for the barest of moments before his lips pressed against mine. On contact, I closed my eyes, giving in to the luxury of the moment.

Holy hell. Frankie Harrison was kissing me.

Our lips brushed together, our mouths parting. Frankie took that as cue to dip in his tongue and sweep against mine. His hand reached into the short strands at the back of my head at the contact. Heat raced along my skin at the touch, tempting me to drag him over the booth so I could get closer.

"Ian!" The tone was aghast and loud, enough to have me pulling away, but not enough to have me remove my gaze from Frankie's. Not yet.

When I finally glanced away, after absorbing the pink in Frankie's cheeks and seeing how breathless he was, my eyes landed on Fredrick.

I frowned and heaved a heavy breath. I was totally busted.

Immediately, my hands flew in the air, placating a wide-eyed Fredrick. "My time is up, the bucket's full, and I'm out of here." The words flew out of me fast, my head still spinning from the taste of Frankie's mouth on mine. Daring to look at the man who'd stolen my breath and rescued me from the vexed Frederick, my stomach plummeted.

He was gone.

What the hell?

Grabbing the bucket and hightailing it out of the booth, I all but rammed the bucket of cash at Fredrick, offering a quick farewell before moving away from the area. Leroy was still lurking. I didn't know if I had any more patience in me today, not with the mind-swirling haze Frankie had left me in.

Finding a safe spot near the cotton candy stall, I stretched out my neck and peered around, desperately trying to remember what color tee Frankie had been wearing.

Blue, like his eyes. Pleased I remembered, I continued my search. I wandered around with no success, mildly aware of people saying hello and me offering them barely there smiles and nods while my gaze didn't give up looking for him.

After fifteen minutes of walking around the place twice, I eventually bumped into Jasper.

"Hey, Ian, where have you been?" He scooted over to me, concern dipping his brows.

"Looking for Frankie." The words spilled out of me, and I regretted them instantly, not quite sure if it was right sharing with him what just happened.

"Frankie?" His scrunched-up face indicated he was thinking. "I haven't seen him for a while. Austin's looking after Tyler for an hour or so, I think, so he won't be far away."

"Okay." I nodded, giving a light shrug, trying to get my wits about me. The reminder of Frankie having a son helped.

A gasp blew past his lips as he raked his gaze over me. "What's wrong? You look all, I don't know... flustered?" He glanced around before returning his attention to me. "Did something happen? You've just finished the booth, right?"

"Yes, and no, I'm fine." A frown dipped my brows when I asked, "Did you invite Leroy?"

Wide-eyed, Jasper shook his head. "Leroy's here? In Kirkby?" He peered intently at me, waiting for me to clarify.

I groaned and closed my eyes before saying, "Yeah, he sure is."

"I didn't invite him. I never speak to the man. How'd he hear about the festival?"

I shrugged. "No idea, but he was all sleazy, trying to shove fifty dollars in the bucket for a kiss."

Jasper scrunched up his nose, making me laugh. That's exactly what I'd wanted to do. "How'd you get out of that?"

I froze, static vibrating in my ears as I considered how to respond. There was no way I wanted to lie to my friend, but I didn't want to tell him about Frankie. While I had no idea if that kiss was simply a friend saving my ass or… not, I still wanted to speak to Frankie to clear the air.

I made to answer, still not sure what to say, when Jasper's name was called out across the crowd. We both swung our heads in that direction. Relief came quickly at the distraction. I seriously owed Austin one.

He headed over to us, Tyler holding his hand and swinging his uncle's arm as he did so. My grin was immediate. This kid was the cutest in his outfit of a nurse's uniform, complete with a unicorn horn and tail and rainbows on his cheeks, I almost melted at the sight.

The cute kid had a hell of a shit start in life with the loss of his mom. While it wasn't any compensation, Frankie had taken to parenting the boy with such impressive ease a couple of years back. It seemed like they'd always been in each other's lives.

I'd spent a fair amount of time with them over the past two years since Frankie moved to the area to be closer to his brother. I visited whenever I got the chance. While the desire for a break from the hospital was all the push I needed to find escape in this small country town, spending time with Jasper was a boon. Obviously, getting to know Frankie and enjoying his company perhaps a little too much may have played a hand in my regular visits.

I was a sucker for punishment.

Austin greeted Jasper with a kiss and me a smile and immediately asked, "Any chance you can look after this little guy until Frankie shows up? He's running late. I have to be at the drag showdown to emcee."

Despite my heart flipping over Frankie being MIA, I smiled, happily agreeing. "We can go have some fun, right, Tyler? Leave the boring grown-ups to go and cause some unicorn mayhem?"

"Yes!" Tyler shouted, jumping once and then all but launching at me. I doubted he knew what "mayhem" meant, but the kid had good taste and liked me, so he'd be up for hanging out.

Austin shot me a grateful smile. "Thanks. I've sent Frankie a text to let him know. If he doesn't run into you, I'm sure he'll call." Jasper told me he'd catch up with me later, and the two of them departed, leaving me alone with a five-year-old who peered at me with expectation in those wide gorgeous blue eyes of his. Ones that were the exact same shade as his dad's.

CHAPTER FOUR

FRANKIE

THE POUNDING IN MY EARS WAS ALL I COULD HEAR. ALL I could focus on. Nothing else mattered except the fast, heavy beating of my heart.

Aimlessly, I walked, not quite sure of the direction but aware there were still lots of people around. My gaze remained dead ahead, not daring to look round and not yet willing to make eye contact with anyone.

When my focus settled on the small makeshift bar, cornered off for adults only, I made a beeline toward it. One beer, and I could use the time to think and get my head straight.

My smile was tight as I nodded in acknowledgment at a few people queueing, and when I was finally served and stepped away to a lone stool at a high table, I swooped on it, perched, and took a large gulp.

As soon as the tangy beer made contact with my tastebuds, I swallowed and exhaled heavily. A small laugh followed, more of a chuckle of disbelief than anything.

I kissed him. Full-on kissed Ian. With tongue.

And holy shit, the taste of him was a whole heap better than the warm beer.

The thing was, there wasn't an ounce of surprise in me at discovering that.

From the first time I'd met Ian, I'd been caught up in his calming presence and gentle smile. And hell, his eyes; just looking into their depths sucked me in. It had taken me one dinner to know I was drawn to the man and wanted to be his friend. It had taken a little over a year to figure out that the ache in my gut whenever we spent time with each other or texted or even I spoke about him to Jasper was actually attraction.

Now, finally, after never thinking I'd get a taste—at least not until he moved to the area—the opportunity had presented itself with his wide-eyed pleas and his mouth that had been begging for more.

And what had I done? Run.

I shook my head and snorted before taking another gulp of beer. My wince this time at the slightly flat liquid not so pronounced.

A beep alerting me to a text had me shifting and pulling my phone out. It was a message from my brother, asking me where I was. *Shit*. I glanced at the time and realized I was late picking up Tyler. Austin had my boy so I could wander around without having to use the eyes in the back of my head. Tyler was a good kid, the best, but hell, if I took my eyes off him for a moment, he had a habit of wandering off, usually in the direction of an animal.

Another message came through, and I paused, amusement bubbling up when I read the words from Austin. It seemed that Ian was looking after Tyler for me.

I had no idea if that was irony or simply serendipitous, or some other fancy word, but it was amusing as hell.

Lifting my plastic cup, I finished off the beer with a new eagerness to seek out my son. The fact that Ian would be there and might decide to hang out with us for the rest of the afternoon added an extra pull for me to find them both.

Dumping my empty cup in the trash, I grinned and took in my surroundings.

No longer was my heart beating erratically, blocking out the loud laughter and conversation of the people around me enjoying the festival. There was definitely a speed to my pulse, but a new excitement pushed the blood flow around for a whole different reason.

It was funny, really, I thought as I wandered around, searching for a glimpse of Ian, that the whole "me running" thing was nothing to do with kissing a man but everything to do with kissing Ian specifically.

The whys of it were as nonsensical as they were real.

Was I straight? No.

Had I openly discussed not being straight? No.

Did I hide any of the above? That was a no too.

So me running was a hundred percent me freaking out about finally kissing the one person who "got me," the one person who I thought I could actually have something real and good with. It took me by surprise.

Possibility was a funny thing that apparently freaked me the fuck out.

Since Ty came into my world and I stepped up two years ago to be his dad—having missed his first three years as I hadn't known he existed—it had forced me to grow up a lot. I'd settled and was building roots in this small town for the first time. I had a job as an office manager in a local law firm, one that wasn't seasonal and about me chasing the party or the next dump of snow as an instructor.

So kissing the man who could change my world again—and I hoped in the best of ways—was mind-blowing. While I imagined it regularly and even planned for it to happen, my fantasies were locked in the future—when he'd finally moved.

Did I want to pursue Ian? Hell yes.

Was I shitting myself? I was touching cloth.

Would I let my worry stop me?

"Daddy."

Immediately my attention shifted to the voice I'd recognize anywhere. I grinned at my blue-eyed boy perched on Ian's shoulders. Ian's gaze was intense, arrowed in on me. That whole sweet nibble he did on his bottom lip, a tell that he was nervous, had me revisiting the question Tyler had pulled me away from.

The answer? No chance in hell would I let my worry stop me. How could I?

Ian doted on my son, had muscles that I was sure could haul me up and throw me around if I so desired, and then there was that whole lip he nibbled, and... damn, the man could kiss.

That he lived hours away posed the same problem. It was one of the main reasons I'd not pounced on the guy over the past year. But there was no way I could forget the heat of his breath mingling with mine. The perfect way his mouth parted and accepted my greedy tongue.

And a kiss like that... yeah, the guy was into me. From the look of concern radiating in my direction as we walked toward each other, it became pretty clear that not pronouncing to the world I wasn't straight, meant he thought I was only into women. Hell, maybe that wasn't it at all, but there was only one way to find out.

I winced internally, figuring me running away wouldn't have helped one iota with that assessment either.

But I never felt the need to say I wasn't straight. One hundred percent, I understood and respected every person who did declare and share part of their identity. Hell, the day my brother came out, I'd been proud as hell.

Until recently—more specifically since becoming a dad—well, me and rules, me and following conventions, expectations, didn't gel all that well.

If I wanted to hook up, I made my intentions clear to that person. If I was attracted to them, I'd be all over that person, regardless of what they packed or how they identified.

And then there was Ian.

The loving, kindhearted guy before me who'd taken me by surprise by making me want something I'd never had before.

"Hey," I greeted once we stood less than a couple of feet from each other. My eyes were on him, aware that Tyler was content perched so high. "Thanks for taking care of Ty for me."

Ian finally released his bottom lip, an action I concentrated on just a little too hard. No longer gnawing, his lip freed, and a small smile curved his lips. "Anytime. Me and Tyler have been having some fun. Isn't that right, kiddo?" Ian's large hands rested gently on my boy's legs, holding him securely. He gave a gentle squeeze when he spoke.

"Sure have, Ian," Ty said, tapping Ian lightly on the head. "We going to see the ladies with pink hair," my boy said excitedly, and my gaze dropped to Ian, who watched me carefully.

I wondered if he expected me to grab my kid and run? As soon as the thought was there, a pang of regret hit me, hating if that was the case. "He okay on your shoulders or do you want me to take him?"

"If you don't want m—"

"No," I said with a shake of my head, cutting him off. "I didn't say I didn't want you." I totally stopped there. His pretty, expressive eyes widened, and like the dick I was, I grinned.

Sure, playing and teasing was so not fair in the moment, but that expression, that pink crawling across his cheeks, it was so worth it.

Just like he was.

"What I'm really asking is do you have to be anywhere, or do you want to hang out with me and Ty? I'd like it a lot if you could come and check out the drag show that's going on."

Ian remained quiet a beat, his eyes holding the same intensity as when I'd first spotted him after I'd run away. His gaze roamed my face. After a beat, and with Tyler fidgeting on his shoulders, Ian finally nodded. "I'd like to hang out with the two of you."

"Perfect." I stepped to his side, squeezing my boy's leg and saying, "No fidgeting when you're so high. You'll fall off and damage the ground."

Tyler peered down at me, his nose wrinkling. "Ian can fix it up. He has superpowers."

I glanced at the man in question. "Have you been training him to say that?"

He laughed. "I think that's all your brother-in-law's doing."

"Hmm." I flicked a glance back up to Ty. "True, his powers are pretty awesome, but some things are more difficult to fix, like dents in the ground, so best be safe, okay?"

"'Kay, Daddy."

Every single time my kid called me that, I swore that my heart melted before reforming bigger than ever before.

We made our way over to the small drag show side by side. Jasper had said something about a competition. It wasn't the destination that held my interest, though, nor the happy, relaxed faces around me, nor even the multitude of rainbow paraphernalia surrounding us. Instead, my attention remained captured by the brush of Ian's arm against mine with every step we took. He hadn't moved away, which sent a shot of awareness through me. There was no doubt he felt the contact, and I hoped that the fact I hadn't run this time, that I was accepting the touch, gave him a good idea of where my headspace was.

The crowds started thickening, not crazily so, but enough that a few missed steps and we could be separated. Instinctively, I reached out and placed my hand in his back pocket, effectively touching his butt, but more specifically not wanting to lose either of them.

His arm jerked a little at the contact, his head shooting around, gaze finding mine.

"This okay?" I asked, angling in so he could hear me. "I don't want to lose you guys."

Something passed in his eyes, and he pursed his lips, which wasn't quite a smile. He nodded. "Sure."

As he slowly angled his face away and our strides slowed to a stop once we had a view of the staging area, I leaned in again, eyeing his hands holding my boy securely. "I liked the idea of holding your hand, but I can keep my jealousy at bay considering you're taking such good care of Ty." I returned my focus to his face as I spoke.

Once more, his gaze was back on me, searching, no doubt looking for clarity if the confused wrinkle between his brows was anything to go by.

"I'm sorry I disappeared back there." I would explain fully later if he gave me the chance, but a deep and meaningful in a crowd now cheering for the couple of sexy drag queens, with my smiling son on Ian's shoulders, wasn't the time. But I wanted to make one thing crystal clear. "I liked kissing you. We can perhaps do it again later. Without the exchange of cash though, if you want?"

I swallowed back the unexpected nerves that took flight as I waited for his response, realizing that legitimately, for the first time in my life, being shot down would hurt. Vulnerability was an odd feeling, something I'd only really experienced when I'd been injured in the motorcycle collision that had killed Ty's mom a couple of years ago.

Now it slammed to the surface, taking my breath from me as I waited.

Ian made the slightest movement of his body, just a couple of inches, angling a little in my direction. His gaze roamed my own before he dipped his head. My eyes sprang wide, realizing his intention. My breath caught when he paused and whispered, "I liked kissing you too."

His lips grazed mine. It was chaste and sweet, though it held the promise of more, especially when a quiet noise—a groan perhaps—slipped past his lips when he pulled away.

By the time he eased back, standing up straight and checking Ty was still secure, his gaze hadn't left mine. And Ty? He was completely oblivious, far too focused on the pretty dresses and the cheering of the crowd.

And me? I wore the biggest shit-eating grin imaginable.

Ian liked my kisses too. That was something we could build on.

CHAPTER FIVE

IAN

THE PAST FOUR HOURS PLAYED ON MY MIND IN A LOOP. I considered every angle, every touch, the twice our mouths had connected, yet my brain buzzed with confusion.

Frankie had just left with Tyler to get him settled for the night. It took everything in me not to latch on like a limpet and say I'd go with him, but that hadn't been tonight's plan. So rather than being with Frankie and tucking in his son, I was at the bar with my friends, trying to relax my muscles and pretend I was enjoying myself.

It sucked, especially because I should be enjoying myself. The atmosphere was incredible, the high of today's success riding the town and the full bar something fierce. Laughter and loud, happy conversation were amplified in the room, and Ted, Jason, Lawrence, and a couple of other staff were run off their feet behind the bar.

"You're quiet tonight," Jasper said from next to me. I pulled my unfocused gaze away from Carter and Billy and a guy, Cody, who I hadn't met before today. They were talking about the drag queen competition.

"I am?" I asked, pleading ignorance.

Jasper's brows dipped low. "Everything okay?"

I nodded immediately. While my head struggled to catch up and make sense of the events of today, if I ignored all of that, I was peachy. How couldn't I be after kissing Frankie so thoroughly that his taste was implanted in me soul deep?

I didn't even have to overthink the reason why that was. I'd crushed on the guy and not so steadily fallen for him from that first time we'd met at Jasper and Austin's for dinner.

"Yeah, all good. Just tired," I said, which wasn't exactly a lie. I'd arrived in town yesterday morning to help set up after only grabbing a couple hours of sleep. I'd worked the night shift, and it had been a busy one.

The situations that some people got themselves into never failed to astound me. For real, when I was on shift, I'd extracted a tooth from an ear canal, tried to convince a guy he wasn't a flying unicorn, which ended up in a debate about what said creature was actually called. I promised him it was an alicorn, but he refused to believe me. My long twelve-hour shift had finished with explaining to a patient why painting your teeth with white nail polish was not a good idea.

Seriously. I could not make this shit up if I tried.

"We can head back early if you want?"

His suggestion raced around inside me. Immediately, my thoughts flicked to Frankie, knowing he was already home. He lived in a brick shed conversion on his brother's property. "Actually, I might just do that, but you guys stay here. I can make my way over. You don't need to call it a night." I planned to leave my car here, since I'd had a few beers.

Jasper's brows dipped, his concern evident. "You sure? I feel kinda bad letting you go back by yourself. Plus there's that hottie Cody over there who Lawrence keeps talking about." He waggled his eyebrows for good measure, making me laugh.

For sure, Cody was a good-looking guy, but the only man on my mind, who'd effectively burrowed himself under my skin over the past two years, was Frankie.

I shook my head and offered Jasper a genuine smile while trying to curb my eagerness. "He's cute for sure, but I'm not interested," I said quietly. "And don't sweat it—me leaving early. It's been a good day. An early night is a luxury."

Jasper stared at me a beat. "Okay. Well, Frankie's around. He'll have put Ty to bed by now, but I'm sure if you need anything, you can just stop by."

The somersault in my stomach had me swallowing hard and made me eager to head off and do just that. "Will do. Just focus on having a good night."

"Sure thing. Go and ask Jason about the transport he's got set up for tonight." He indicated toward my finished beer bottle.

I smiled, letting him know I would.

After accepting Jasper's friendly hug goodbye, I made my way over to Jason. I caught his attention with a finger lift while he served someone. As soon as he was done, he headed over with a small smile.

"Ian, what can I get you?"

"I'm actually looking at heading out early. Is there a chance you can organize a ride? I know it's not even nine."

"Sure. Everything good? Heard you made an impression at the booth." He quirked his brow at me, an amused smile on his face.

My eyes widened, wondering if he knew, if he'd seen. "Uhm…."

He shook his head, leaning forward, arms on the polished bar top. "I happened to be walking past. Anyone else know?"

"No," I answered, heat filling my cheeks.

"Frankie's already at home, right? Putting his kid to bed or something?"

When I nodded, he smirked, but I didn't miss the creasing of his forehead. "Just be careful, all right?"

My brows lifted high, my stomach bottoming out a little. "Careful?"

Jason hesitated and pursed his lips, seeming to debate something. "It's nothing. Just me being over-protective. You're both good guys. I'm sure you'll figure it out." He rapped the bar with his knuckles. "Head outside. The car will be there in five."

I said my thanks and walked outside, my stomach churning with nerves. As soon as fresh air hit me, I looked out, my gaze landing on my current pain in the ass.

Leroy.

His gaze immediately latched on to mine. Somehow I managed to hold back my groan of frustration. I was still clueless why he'd come all this way to a small-town festival. Sure, he'd asked me out, but this was a bit much if I was the reason.

Leroy approached like a twitchy weasel, a smile that made my skin crawl on his face. Even though I wasn't exactly a short guy, he loomed over me. But what I lacked in height, I made up in the pounds I was packing.

Working out, going to the gym was my only real outlet. It helped me shrug off my manic days and sometimes the shitshows I encountered. And while my muscle mass was often advantageous both at work and when looking to get laid, at that moment, I wished I wasn't quite conspicuous.

There was something behind Leroy's eyes that made me shudder on the inside, and if I wasn't so used to dealing with weirdos and stressful situations, it would have been a whole-body shiver.

Leroy's gaze flickered over me, fast at first, then a slow roam that made me shudder. No words were spoken as he perused me, his tongue peeking out and wetting his bottom lip.

I pulled my gaze away, searching for the car Ted had arranged to chauffer partygoers around for a low fee. With no vehicle yet in sight, I sighed, succumbing to the inevitable of speaking to the man.

Sometimes my politeness was a curse. But I struggled to be any other way.

The weasel-looking man took a step closer. Not so close that he was in my personal space, but still too close for my liking. "Ian, I was just thinking about you."

Despite myself, I shot him a tight smile.

"Out for some fresh air, or are you looking to take the party elsewhere?"

"I'm done for the night so am heading back."

"If you're looking for compa—"

I cut him off immediately. "I'm not."

The look in his eyes didn't shift. "I'm sure I can persuade you otherwise."

I shook my head. "I'm good, thanks."

"Just good?" He pouted. "That won't do. I can turn that into great."

Lights appeared at the end of the street, and I hoped like hell it was my ride. This time I had no response, my gaze intent on the approaching lights. A shuffle and movement, and Leroy had encroached on my space.

"I like that you keep playing hard to get."

I grimaced and shook my head. "That's not what I'm doing. I'm just not interested."

"But all of these muscles—" He reached out a hand and trailed his fingers over my right pec. I backed away immediately, not wanting his hands anywhere near me. "—they're clearly made to be admired." He took a step closer, and this time I stood my ground. "Worshipped."

The car was slowing, but I was reluctant to remove my gaze from the sleaze before me.

It was times like these when I wished I had that trigger that would occasionally snap so I could punch someone, make the words they refused to hear crystal clear when my fist connected with their face.

Too many times similar situations like this had happened to me. One just a few years back was how I ended up meeting Davis and Scott. Maybe some guys had a fetish for built men. I hadn't a clue. All I knew was that I hated violence after seeing so many injuries in the ER and too many victims of one-punch deaths.

I was strong and could probably bench press Leroy without breaking a sweat. Even if he did push me, I had no desire to hurt the guy to a point where he couldn't walk away from injury.

When the car stopped, I exhaled in relief and side-stepped Leroy.

His hand clasping my arm stopped me.

"You're seriously going to walk away after I came all this way because of you?"

I eyed where he gripped, and when he didn't release, I pulled. The jolt did the job, and he was forced to drop his hand. Angled half toward him, I said, "I don't even know how you knew about the festival or who invited you, but it wasn't me. I'm not interested."

All at once, his expression morphed. A gleam appeared in his eyes. He was pissed off. "What's your problem? It's not like you've got anywhere better to be or anyone better to be with. You should feel lucky I'm paying you any interest." He scoffed, his eyes narrowing. "You're a nurse, for Christ's sake. It's not—"

"You need to back off, right now, asshole."

I had a moment to appreciate Leroy's eyes shooting wide open before jerking my gaze in the direction of the voice.

Frankie.

His car door was open, and he was striding in my direction, looking fierce and generally all handsome and chivalrous.

My heart flipped over several times in a row, and when I took in the expression in his eyes and just how worked up he was, my stomach joined in and somersaulted.

When Frankie looked like this, I had no qualms with him going into this sexy, protective mode. It was hot, and while I had no idea how Leroy was responding behind me, I didn't care, because Frankie was here.

I didn't know why or how, but I was ridiculously pleased he was.

Rather than brushing past me and getting in Leroy's grill, he stopped before me, so close his breath swept across my face.

"You okay?"

I grinned, the precarious situation of a few moments ago already shoved to the side. "Yeah." I nodded. "You're here?" The question was evident in my voice.

"Yeah. Marcy, Carter's mom, offered to have Ty. She was already looking after Libby, Davis and Scott's girl. So I collected Ty's overnight things and took him to Davis's, got him settled in before coming back here to be with you."

"We were in the middle of something. Do you mind?" Leroy's voice took me by surprise. So caught up in Frankie and knowing he'd come back for me, I'd all but forgotten about the annoyance of Leroy.

While Frankie's gaze narrowed, it didn't pull away from me as he asked, "That the same guy from today?"

I nodded and rolled my eyes. "Yeah. It seems like the word *no* just doesn't compute."

Leroy started talking behind me, and it sounded like he'd moved, but my focus stayed on Frankie, whose anger resurfaced.

"Maybe he'll finally get a clue now and fuck off before he gets my size elevens up his ass."

I grinned while also thinking about his foot size and wondering if that would translate to his dick. Not that a long dick necessarily did it for me. I was a firm believer in action and performance rather than size.

Frankie quirked a brow at me. "Do I want to know what you're thinking?"

"Huh?"

His lips quirked. "Was it something dirty?"

I barked out a laugh but didn't get the chance to respond as Leroy moved into my line of vision. A huff of breath escaped me that he was still here. Reluctantly I turned in his direction.

His weasel-like features were narrow and focused intently on me.

"You didn't tell me you were with someone," he grouched, and it took everything I had not to flip him off.

Frankie didn't seem to have the same hang-ups as me as he reached out and took my hand in his. "I don't know what it is you think you're doing, but it's time you got a clue and backed off. When a guy says no but is too polite to tell you to fuck off, show some respect and do the right thing," he said, his tone deceptively calm and doing all sorts of things to my heart rate. "While Ian here may not say it, I have no hardship in doing it. He's with me, he's not inter-ested, and this is the last time he or I should be telling you to back off for good. Understood?"

And there went my cock springing to life, thickening up, embarrassingly so in my jeans.

"You're really going to let this guy speak for you?" Leroy said to me with a sneer.

I quirked my brow, surprised at how relaxed I felt despite the confrontation. "Since I already spoke for myself and told you no too many times to count, I've no issues with Frankie giving you the same message, albeit a little more honestly."

I didn't have it in me to care that Leroy was now flushing red and that there was another shift in his eyes. No longer was it a look that gave me the creeps, but I finally believed Frankie's words had sunk in, once and for all.

I was a caretaker by nature. It was my strength as well as my weakness at times. It had certainly come back and bit me on the ass.

Leroy's "Sorry" took me by surprise, and as if he knew I was going to respond with an "okay," Frankie tightened his grip on my hand, pulling my attention to him. A subtle shake of his head. He'd definitely read my intention.

He was right. None of Leroy's attention or behavior was okay. With this in mind, I clamped my mouth shut, refusing to give Leroy an out, and instead watched him leave.

A moment later, Frankie and I were blissfully alone, and I inhaled a deep breath and exhaled, happy Frankie had shown up when he did.

"So—"

A car pulling up cut him off, and I realized it was my ride. "Shit, that's for me."

"Where were you going?"

Tugging my bottom lip into my mouth, I mulled over my answer before going for "I was coming to see you."

The smile that lifted his lips high was spectacular. He was attractive all the time, but with a smile like this, he was crazy hot.

"You want to apologize and let him know you won't be needing his services, and I'll drive?"

My nod was immediate. "I can do that," I said, my voice breathy.

In less than a couple of minutes, we drove to his place. Not only was he child-free, but his brother wasn't home either. Knowing we would be alone, combined with the rush of desire from Frankie looking out for me with Leroy, was a heady thing.

I'd thought his big smile made him hot, but that unexpected dominance he'd weaved through his voice, threaded with his no-bullshit tone, had been sexy as hell.

I wanted nothing more than to see where this thing went between us. Sure, I had a whole list of questions buzzing through my brain, but I was at the point of not caring about any of the answers.

Instead, all I wanted was another kiss.

CHAPTER SIX

FRANKIE

IT WAS RARE SOMEONE GOT MY BACK UP. IT WAS EVEN rarer for me to step into a situation and come close to punching a guy. But from the body language alone—Ian's had screamed of discomfort—I'd been on high alert. And then when I'd heard some of the bullshit spewing out of the dickhead's mouth, pissed off wasn't close to the level of anger surging to the surface.

I was fucking livid.

Consent was a gift, and anyone who messed with that and refused to listen deserved to be castrated. And with the douche's attention so focused on Ian, legit, the sweetest man I knew, I'd come seriously close.

I side-eyed the man beside me, listened to his

breathing in the quiet car. Nerves all but radiated off him, and I couldn't pinpoint if there was a particular reason or a multitude. Either way, I could list off the potential causes for the tension. And I got it. Seriously I did.

When I'd scored a babysitter, my plan had hit me with renewed need to see Ian and clear the air and hopefully get some more action going. That he'd been on his way to see me did all sorts of things to my heart while simultaneously muddling my brain.

But I didn't want to talk it out in the car. When we spoke about the heavier stuff, I wanted to see his face, read his reaction. Only then could I be sure we were on the same page.

One thing for certain was Ian had no poker face. His emotions, his feelings were always laid bare for those who looked closely enough. And I certainly focused a lot on the man.

He was too pretty for his own good. The combination of his expressive eyes with his sweet smile, right along with his defined body, made the man a wet dream. Once you merged those traits with how caring and funny he was, it made him a *dangerous* wet dream.

Since it was rare I backed away from danger, I had no desire to run from that lethal combination.

Not anymore.

Despite the quiet and the thrum of awareness, comfort settled between us. Over the years, I'd blurred the lines of friendship a time or two, but this was different. I wasn't naïve to the fact that Ian was special.

We'd been good friends for some time, and while I didn't want that to change, the pull in my gut, the nudge in my heart whispering to me that we could be so much more was impossible to ignore. Today, that kiss had changed everything.

I continued to mull that over, considered a future with a steady boyfriend, wondered about the possibility of Tyler having two parents who adored him.

There was little doubt Ian already doted on him. He was a rare breed of man who spent time with kids, even those not blood-related, and drew pure joy from doing so. Knowing he'd be an excellent dad sent me a fresh jolt of awareness.

This could be it. Serious. The one.

While I'd had the past year to reflect on the fact, I'd not considered how we'd get to this point without simply laying it out for him, which clearly I hadn't done. Yet.

I grinned as we pulled up in the driveway, thinking about the dickhead Leroy. To see his reaction if he ever discovered he was responsible for finally putting the two of us in a position to drop all pretense of only friendship would be awesome.

"Anything in particular you're grinning about over there?" Ian's question drew my gaze to him as I switched off the ignition.

Those pretty eyes snagged my attention immediately. God, I wanted this man as much as a parent wanted just ten minutes' peace.

"Just wondering how that dipshit would react, knowing he's the reason we're here. I think I should find his address and send him a thank-you card or something."

A light chuckle fell from Ian, and I reached out and unbuckled my seat belt and then his. As though acting on its own accord, the desire to touch him riding me hard, my hand snaked up his neck, and I cupped his cheek. When his breath caught, I tilted my head, my gaze never wavering from his face.

"Are you okay to come to my place or…?" I trailed off, not really wanting to give him an out, but knowing I absolutely needed to.

"Yours is good. I don't think Jasper and Austin will be back for a while."

My brows dipped in at the mention of my brother and his best friend. The truth was, I hadn't given them a second thought. I hadn't really considered anyone else's reaction, which I begrudgingly admitted was one of my traits of old, one I wasn't quite so proud of. While I liked to think being a dad had changed me, I was far from perfect, and some habits were hard to break.

"Do you think this is going to be a problem for them?" I asked, genuinely curious rather than concerned.

Ian rested a hand on top of mine against his cheek and leaned into it a little. "Surprised, maybe."

I nodded at his words, agreeing he was probably right.

"You need me to explain things to you before we head on inside?" I offered, mentally high fiving myself at the courtesy.

"Any reason why we can't do that inside?"

I brushed my thumb across his bottom lip and asked, "Truth?"

With a nod, he answered, "Always."

"The last thing I plan to be doing with you when inside is talking. I can think of better uses for both our mouths."

His gulp was audible in the quiet car.

When he remained silent, I offered, "Or we can do the whole talk thing in the morning?"

"Yes," he said, both quickly and breathily, making me laugh. His chuckle soon joined in, and his smile stretched his mouth wide. "Yeah," he said, this time more together and controlled. "I'm good with talking tomorrow morning if you are."

"Definitely." I pulled away, not wanting to kiss him in the cramped space. I opened the door and heard him doing the same thing. We met at the back of the car, his hand immediately reaching out for me. With clasped hands and adrenaline riding me, we headed toward my home.

I kept my gaze on the door, figuring a quick look at him would unravel me and I'd end up clinging to him outside, which would make one heck of an alternative garden statue for Austin's headlights to shine on.

The outside lights along the small pathway were on, creating soft shadows that moved in the gentle spring breeze. We followed the pebbled route while I adjusted my keys in my hand to find the door key. It didn't take long before we were in the house and in the open-plan space, looking at each other, still hand in hand.

Once I dropped my keys in the ceramic pot one of my sisters had gifted me, I tugged Ian toward me. He came willingly, a slight curve of his lips lifting his mouth as he did so.

"So you said earlier something about more kisses."

"I did that."

Ian's eyes remained glued to mine. "You can make good on that now if you want?"

I barely had time to respond, let alone react to his request before he leaned toward me, pressed himself against my body, and wrapped an arm around my waist.

Hell, I liked him like this, going for it, taking what he wanted, and I was so on board for more mouth action.

He pressed his lips against mine.

I lost my breath, lost thoughts of anything beyond this man and how perfectly his mouth moved against mine.

My world shifted. It had previously tilted just a few short hours ago, but this was something different, more significant somehow. Need pooled in my gut, racing quickly through my body and making me hard and ache for anything and everything Ian was willing to give. All thoughts of holding back, which was precisely what I'd done this past year, melted away as his tongue dipped into my mouth, caressing and tangling and tasting so delicious.

Christ, I wanted to time travel and punch myself for not doing this sooner. If only I'd acted the first time the depth of my feelings became clear, we wouldn't have wasted all this time.

I stepped forward so Ian's butt found purchase on the back of the couch. Immediately, he spread his legs so I could stand between his thighs. The muscles there pressed against my legs, sending a thrill straight to my dick. I broke free from our kiss. "Fuck, I can't wait to see you naked."

His smile was sweet, his eyes half-mast when he hauled my mouth back to him.

He ghosted his tongue against my lips. I opened once again, eager for every touch.

I liked kissing, but *like* didn't even come close to how much I loved what Ian was giving me—his quiet strength, his familiarity, his certainty.

It was the latter that was one hell of a turn-on.

I groaned when he deepened the kiss, and I pushed against him, wishing we were already naked and in my bedroom.

I cast an errant thought to my room and condoms, not sure I actually had any. Lube, I had an impressive collection, but in the last couple of years, the need for a condom in my bedside drawer wasn't something I'd had to worry about.

Needing to address this now before I was too far gone to think straight, I pulled away. The movement earned me a disgruntled groan.

"Are you trying to kill me? You keep taking your mouth away."

I chuckled and rubbed my groin against him, punishing myself as much as Ian. "Sorry, but condoms, do you have any?"

Dragging his bottom lip through his teeth, he nodded. The simple action and knowledge we were covered almost had me unraveling and dropping to my knees now. My bed sounded like a much better place for this, though.

"Perfect. Come with me." With his hand in mine, I led him to my bedroom. Once there, I flicked on the small floor lamp and stalked toward him. I needed him naked. Stat.

"Can I undress you?" I asked, need pitching my voice low.

"Absolutely." A gulp followed the single word, and his body practically quivered as I removed each item of clothing with gentle caresses and perfectly placed kisses.

Delicious whimpers and groans spilled from him, and when I licked down his abs that had kept me awake one too many nights, he heaved out a heavy sigh.

"You doing okay?"

"Yeah." His Adam's apple bobbed. "No one's ever undressed me before," he admitted.

I peered up at him from my knees, taking in the sexy man before me. "You like it?"

"I like you doing it."

Happiness flooded through my chest at his words. Here I was on my knees before this incredible guy, and in doing so, making him feel good. It was the best high I'd ever had.

Snowboarding and doing a triple flip, hell, skydiving had nothing on the rush of adrenalin from giving this man everything he deserved.

"Shall we take this to the bed?" I asked, a hairsbreadth from his jerking cock.

He hesitated a moment before he nodded. "I want you to be comfortable, so yeah." He then grinned, adding, "And naked; definitely naked."

I gave one long lick and suck, just because I couldn't resist, before standing and making fast work of my clothes.

Ian used the time to grab his wallet, and I watched as he tugged out two condoms, placing them on the bed. I grinned and made my way over to collect the lube.

Naked, hard, and with supplies, I was on him as soon as he backed onto the bed.

No more waiting.

CHAPTER SEVEN

IAN

IT HAD BEEN A WHILE SINCE I LAST TOPPED, BUT AFTER Frankie tormented me with foreplay until I was certain I would lose my mind, I didn't even hesitate when he asked me to roll on the condom and get him ready.

As I prepped him, I didn't know where to look. I was desperate for his gaze, loved the sensation of being caught in his snare, but then my fingers working him over. Him greedily sucking me in was a vision I had no desire to forget anytime soon, let alone look away from.

"Okay, please," he said with a soft, almost desperate sigh, "I'm ready."

I paused, and my gaze shot to his face, brows high in surprise. Hours of fantasies had been stored in my mind about Frankie, but this side of him that was finally coming out—the desperate and needy requests and sounds he made—it blew all my expectations out of the ballpark.

He was so much more than I ever envisioned.

Loud, confident, and a little cocky, Frankie was my opposite in so many ways. I loved those traits, but beneath me, legs spread and raised, a pillow under his hips, there was a vulnerability to the man that took my breath away.

I liked it. A lot.

And as much as I'd love to tease and drag this out, I'd been ready for the past two years for this moment. I refused to wait another.

Slathering myself with lube, I focused on his reaction rather than the need pulsating through me. I wanted to get off something fierce and was sure I'd blow quickly once I sank into his heat, but I needed him to lose control. Wanted him to explode so damn hard he'd see stars.

Before pressing into him, I leaned close and brushed my mouth against his, sighing in contentment and barely restrained when he looped his arms around me and took the kiss deeper.

Pulling away, I lined myself up. "You good?"

Eyes blazing with a new intensity, he nodded. "Yes. I'll be even better as soon as you're inside me."

My smile was soft, mirroring his own when I worked my way past his tight ring, pausing and pulling out an inch before pushing forward. The groan escaping Frankie's lips made me still. Immediately, his eyes sprang open, and he grabbed my waist.

"Don't stop."

I hesitated, searching his eyes for the truth.

"It's just been a while since I was impaled, and I don't think ever by a cock as fat as yours."

Amusement warred with my concern, his words not reassuring me. "You want to swap? I don't mind bottoming," I offered. While it was the last thing my dick wanted—to pull out of the snug channel—I absolutely would in a heartbeat.

With an unrelenting grip, Frankie flexed his fingers and squeezed around me.

"Fuck," I groaned, slipping in another inch without intending to.

"No stopping. I want this, you inside me."

"Impaling you?" I said, revisiting his words and chuckling, despite my slightly hazy vision and the building heat.

He laughed, making us both wince. "Impale away, Ian."

With a smirk, I did just that.

I kept my gaze on him the whole time, adjusting to his reactions and focusing so damn hard on his pleasure while wishing like hell that I had a cock ring.

"You want to jack yourself?" I asked as I pulled out, only to push back inside him, angling my hips in a way his cries of pleasure told me he liked.

He shook his head, eyes glazed and voice wispy when he said, "No. I'll come."

"Thank fuck," I said, picking up my speed and wiping the momentary laugh and smile from his face.

When my balls tightened, I grunted, wishing I had it in me to hold off. But Frankie felt too good, too perfect. His hands were everywhere, his gasps and sighs the best background noise to my steady pounds, and every time he cursed and demanded more, I flicked my hips. My gaze slipped out of focus when he tightened around me and cried out as I nailed his prostate.

No way could I wait.

My hand gripped his length. He was hot and hard, and I couldn't wait until I got the chance to ride him.

With that thought joining the pleasure spiraling up my spine, I grunted. "Oh, fuck." The words spilled out a moment before my release. I jerked and shuddered, my hand moving, my brain not quite functioning.

"Fuck. My dick."

I zeroed in on Frankie's words, becoming aware of my coated hand. I huffed out a chuckle and eased off before pulling out of him and taking care of the condom.

"Here." He passed me a couple of tissues from the bedside table, and I wrapped the latex up and dropped it on the floor. He gave me another to wipe my hand as he cleared his stomach. A moment later, he took the used tissues from me, threw them on the floor with his, and hauled me to his side.

I went willingly, sighing contently and burying my face against his neck.

Most guys I'd been with, who were admittedly one-night stands, tended not to be into the whole cuddle thing. But I loved it. Snuggling up against a warm body, the scent of sex still on our skin—there was something both heady and sexy about it.

Combine that with the man being Frankie, who wrapped his arms around me and tugged me close, it was officially the best night ever.

I knew we were due a conversation in the morning, but connected as we were, there was no foreboding, no hesitation about what would be said.

How could there be when I was more and more convinced that we were perfect for each other? And if he gave me a chance, I'd do everything in my power to make him see it.

The pounding on the front door woke us both up.

"Shit, what time is it?" Frankie sat bolt upright and scrambled for his phone. A frown appeared on his forehead. "It's only just turned eight. Hell, I thought I'd overslept to pick up Tyler."

Just as I was about to ask what time that was, there were four more loud raps on the door.

"Urgh. I suppose I best go and answer that. If it's Austin or Jasper, I'm surprised they haven't let themselves in already."

Those words brought a fresh wave of awareness of our situation, and I joined him in his upright position. Wide-eyed, I looked at the man beside me. "It'll be Jasper. He'll be freakin' out that I wasn't in bed this morning."

"How would he know? Wouldn't he be expecting you to have a lie-in or something?"

I snorted. "Jasper's a morning person. You know this."

He laughed. "True."

"He's also the ultimate host and usually brings me up a cup of coffee."

Frankie's eyes widened. "Seriously? I never got coffee in bed when I was staying there."

His indignation was sweet and caused me to smirk. "What can I say? I'm his favorite."

Frankie launched himself at me, pressing me flat across the mattress and kissing my smile clean off me. I sighed into the kiss, luxuriating in the contact and how normal all this was.

The door banged again.

"Shit," Frankie said. "I really can't ignore it for the third time." With that, he pulled away, which was kinda sad until my gaze landed on his bare ass. It was one hell of a perfect morning view, and I was disappointed when he tugged on a pair of boxers.

"You're going to answer the door in those?" I asked, wondering how he looked so sexy having woken up just a couple of minutes ago.

He waggled his brows up and down. "These will help scare Jasper off," he said with a laugh. "Means I can get back to bed to you sooner."

Warmth heated my chest. I liked that possibility a lot, but as I watched him, I sighed, knowing it was unlikely to happen. If it was Jasper worried about me, I needed to show my face.

While I didn't know yet what was happening between me and Frankie, and we hadn't yet had that talk, I wasn't prepared to hide away in his room. Nor did I expect Frankie to do that either.

Rather than simply slipping my boxers back on, I tugged on my jeans and T-shirt. It was a necessary evil to not give Jasper too much of an eyeful this morning.

When I headed closer to the main living space, I heard Frankie's voice. While I couldn't hear what he was saying, his tone was light, normal. I exited the small hallway, my gaze landing on first Frankie, then not only Jasper but Austin as well.

Austin's focus was immediately on me, followed swiftly by Jasper's.

Jasper's jaw dropping would have been comical if not for the concern evident in his eyes.

"Oh, okay. You're here?" He pitched it as a question and gave me an assessing look before doing the same to Frankie. "Right, well, uhm… I made breakfast."

I cast a glance at Austin. His brows were dipped low, his focus entirely on his brother, who simply stood there, appearing super nonchalant and as though the atmosphere hadn't shifted and become weird, verging on awkward.

"Excellent," Frankie said. "We're going to need half hour or so here first, then we'll come over. Will breakfast wait or…?" His tone remained casual, and I was almost certain he wasn't faking it. That knowledge swept over me, giving me confidence and dampening the small ball of unease building in my gut when I'd seen Jasper and Austin.

"Sure, yeah, no problem. It can wait." Jasper's response was directed at Frankie, but before he prodded at his boyfriend's stomach, indicating they should leave, he shot me a look that had my lips twitching. With his brows high, he mouthed, "What the fuck?" I contained the bubble of amusement at this whole meeting, figuring that particular emotion was so much better than freaking out or overthinking.

My shrug didn't score me any brownie points, if I interpreted his narrowed eyes accurately.

Sure, as his best friend, I had some explaining to do, should I so choose, and I was okay with that. Of course, that would come after Frankie and I talked things through.

Frankie showed them out, and it hadn't gone unnoticed that Austin had remained mute during the whole exchange. They didn't know exactly what had gone down last night, but when I took in Frankie's appearance that screamed thoroughly fucked, with his ruffled hair, his lazy grin, and the stubble rash on his neck and his chin, even from a few yards away, I was sure their assumptions were on the money.

"You look like you could do with some coffee." Frankie headed toward me, his gaze lingering on my own before he perused my body. "I would have liked you to be naked for a little while longer." Disappointment filtered through his light tone, and I couldn't help but agree.

In the brightness of the morning light, and before we continued, I needed to know where his thoughts lay, specifically whether last night was a one-night thing or not. While last night it had seemed to the contrary, I wasn't a stranger to words spoken in the heat of the moment and the false promises that often accompanied them.

"And us being naked, do you see that happening again?" I aimed for casual, not quite sure I pulled it off. Frankie's wrinkled brow and tightening jaw suggested he read me too easily.

I hoped that was a good thing.

Once in front of me, Frankie reached out and threaded his fingers through one of the belt loops on my jeans. He exerted a little pressure and used it to pull me snug to his body. This was a connection I liked a lot.

"I'd like us being naked together as often as possible, just like I want us to hang out as often as possible and explore this thing between us."

I exhaled a quiet, long breath, my shoulders releasing some of their tightness. "I'd like that too, and I know Ty's in that mix as well."

Frankie's eyes lit up at my words. They were bright and intense as they captured my gaze. "He already thinks you're Thor, you know, the short-haired version."

I grinned widely, loving that his kid thought I was the badass god of thunder. Obviously, besides my physique, I was nothing at all like Chris Hemsworth. A guy could wish, but since Frankie seemed to like my face and my whole package so much, I could more than cope with that reality.

"Ty's an intelligent boy," I said with a chuckle.

"He is that." Frankie punctuated his response with a small kiss before leading me to the kitchen and caffeine. "You want a shower or something? We can always shower up after breakfast. There should be enough time before picking Ty up."

"After's fine. I can then grab my bag and toiletries from their spare room." The thrill of knowing I'd be bringing my things back here bubbled in awareness.

Frankie nodded as he busied himself making coffee. After organizing the mugs, he turned to face me as I leaned with my back against the countertop opposite him. He mirrored my stance.

"So, I'm assuming you have questions."

That was the thing, I really did, but honestly, he didn't owe me an explanation about his sexuality. I'd be happy to hear his story if he wanted to share, would really like to, in fact. I'd learned long ago that our journeys were our own, though, and as long as we were true to ourselves, and hopefully didn't tell bare-faced lies or hurt others in the process, I was good with that.

With all this jumbling through my mind, I settled on "Only if you want to share. After last night, after what you've just said, that's all I need to know. Sure, I'm curious," I admitted, aware my cheeks heated, "but I don't think you owe me an explanation about your past." I gave a one-shoulder shrug before adding, "Over the past couple of years, I think we've become good friends, right?"

"We have," he said immediately.

I nodded and offered him a genuine smile, feeling the truth of his words gut-deep. "And I think we know each other well. We've shared plenty about our pasts. Sure, not everything, but it's a damn sight more groundwork than anyone I've ever been with, any relationship I've ever had," I clarified, figuring I'd make my hopes clear.

He looked at me with an intensity that had me pausing. "What?" I asked, nonplussed.

Frankie gave the slightest shake of his head, gaze still intent. "It's just, I've seriously never met anyone like you before."

I grinned, a zip of awareness shooting straight to my heart at his words. "This level of fabulous is pretty rare," I joked.

While he smiled at my words, there was a soft seriousness in the gaze he directed my way. "It is." He poured our coffees, preparing mine how I liked it without asking. That he was able to do so was sweet. While he'd made me plenty of cups, now it just seemed... more. "Couch?" he asked, and I nodded, taking my drink off him with thanks and making my way to the comfortable soft leather.

The room was comfortable, welcoming. It was also a mix of masculine combined with a toy store. The combination always had me relaxing. Now was no different.

After sitting, I blew on the steaming liquid, took a tentative sip, and placed it on the small table off to the side.

"Asbestos mouth," Frankie said with a chortle and a shake of his head. "I have no idea how you can even take a small sip when it's so damn hot."

I grinned. "Years of having no breaks at work and grabbing a swig of coffee, even when scalding, whenever the chance came. It has a numbing effect." For the past ten years, double shifts, crazy, often manic days (and nights) at my job meant I was used to doing basic tasks, like shoving a sandwich in my mouth and inhaling caffeine at super speed. It was a pitfall of my profession, and while I was at peace with that, I hoped one day to take it a little easier, find an even quieter hospital to work at.

"I can't even imagine," he responded, his intense gaze on me. "You work your ass off."

I shrugged in acknowledgment. "I just do my bit."

"And some," he added, his praise making my cheeks warm.

"Are you still looking for a new position?"

I nodded slowly, my eyes assessing, wondering if he was asking because of us. The thought sent a shot of hope through my chest. "Yeah. I've put in my résumé everywhere close by." Frankie knew this. I'd spoken about it often enough. Over the past few years, my friendship group had grown and somehow landed here in this small community, a long way away from my roots. And I'd happily chase that, wanting a home where I was supported and accepted.

Sure, there was plenty of nightlife in the city, but it was easy to become lost in the place of many, become faceless and insignificant.

When in my twenties, it was what I'd wanted, but now, encroaching on my midthirties, I was ready for so much more.

"And still no joy?" His disappointed voice sent fresh emotion to roll .

"Not yet, but I've become friendly with a few staff around the hospital close by and the different medical offices. As soon as something comes up, I know I'll be contacted." I was nothing if not persistent. I made it my mission to contact the local hospital covering the three small towns every two or three weeks, reminding them I was keen.

"That's good. Something will become available."

I picked up my coffee and took a swig, waiting to see if he was going to open up or not.

"I can see your brain ticking over," he said, a small smirk forming.

"Is that so?"

"Yeah, I do okay at reading you."

I snorted, knowing he spoke the truth, though I did wonder if he was so good at reading me, whether he'd known all this time I'd been panting over him.

"So, yeah, I'm not straight," he said matter-of-factly, completely changing the subject. "The first time I was with a guy was at college."

I took that in, confusion sweeping through me. Everything I knew about Frankie—before yesterday at least—told me he was a straighter shooter, both in speaking the truth as well as his sexuality.

"From your frown, I'm going to take a stab in the dark that you're wondering why you didn't know."

"There's that—and Austin?" The look Austin had cast his brother earlier suggested he was as befuddled as I was yesterday.

"I've never said I was straight. Never said I was not straight."

My brows dipped low at those two statements.

"It makes me sound like a flippant asshole, right?" A self-deprecating huff of a laugh followed.

"Are you?" I asked, the question tumbling out.

His stare pierced me, a new sort of intensity in his gaze. The slight shake of his head preceded his words: "It wasn't my intention, no. LGBTQ visibility is important. I believe it, respect it. Every single person, friend or otherwise, who I've met over the years, my brother included, who has come out and identified as being in the community, I'm fucking proud of." He tilted his head, seemingly examining my reaction as my brows remained drawn low. His smile was soft as he continued. "I'm not ashamed. I simply choose not to have a label. I know some people don't get or even respect that, and honestly, they can go fuck themselves."

I snorted at his words, beginning to understand his mindset.

"Some people I know assume I'm gay, or bi, or pan, you know? They've seen me flirting and hooking up with different kinds of people of different genders, different sexualities. It's just that Austin and everyone in this small community haven't seen me hook up with anyone. Sure, they know about Ty's mom, so I understand the assumption."

"Until me." The words were quieter and breathier than I intended, but hell, he'd been living here for two years and had pretty much told me in all that time he hadn't hooked up once. I was the only guy. Was it wrong that *that* detail had zoomed to the fore-front of my mind rather than everything else he shared?

"Until you," he agreed, reaching out and stroking his thumb across my cheek before he settled his hand on my shoulder. The touch was warm and familiar. "I think it's safe to say that both Austin and Jasper have figured out that I'm into you."

"Is that what this is?" I asked, my gaze roaming his face. "This is you being into me?"

"Well, technically, you were the one balls deep inside me last night," he sassed, his grin mischievous.

"Ha!" I shook my head, ignoring the twitch of my dick at his words. He'd still yet to return the favor, and honestly, I was keen to change that as soon as he wanted. I rarely topped, much preferring to release control and bottom, but I happily took anything Frankie was willing to give yesterday.

Half-lidded eyes focused on me. "You want me inside you, Ian?"

My cock perked up immediately, and I swallowed hard. It would be so easy to make that happen right now, especially as all this time Frankie remained just in his boxer briefs, leaving little to the imagination. Not that I needed to rely on that, though. Last night I'd thoroughly acquainted myself with his dick.

I dragged my gaze away from his crotch, where he was thickening out, and tried to get my mind back on track, even if it was for a little while. "I really do," I admitted. My words made him smile and adjust himself, and I groaned. "But your brother and my best friend are waiting. Plus, you have to pick up Ty."

Frankie huffed out a long breath and tilted his head back.

"You okay?"

"Uh-huh. Just counting."

I laughed. I should probably have done the same thing.

When he returned his focus to me with a tender look, my laughter petered off. Along with the tenderness, there was an unexpected seriousness in his expression.

"Listen," he started, "I didn't mean to confuse you about me or my attraction. Truth is, I've liked you for a while."

"You have?" Surprise colored my words. I hadn't picked up on that at all. Well, other than that moment last night. Sure we'd spent a decent amount of time with each other, and we flirted. But honestly, the guy was a flirt with almost everyone he met. We even texted and chatted on the phone every now and then, but I'd never picked up an interested vibe. In my defense, I hadn't been looking for it—too afraid of being disappointed if I didn't see it.

"I really have. About a year ago," he admitted, "was the first time I admitted to myself you're sexy as fuck and I wanted to explore something beyond friend-ship with you."

Heat flushed my body, fast and wild at his words. "A whole year?" I shook my head. "Why didn't you act on it?" Once again, my open questions surprised the heck out of me, but since this was Frankie, who I genuinely considered one of my closest friends, embarrassment didn't lick at my skin.

"Honestly?" His thumb was back to stroking my skin, and I nodded. "Part of it was the newness of me being a dad and not wanting to do anything to screw with that." I totally understood why that would have been a concern. The last two years hadn't been a cakewalk for him. "You living where you do and what that would mean if we tried something held me back as well."

I grimaced. "Where I live hasn't changed."

"True, but before yesterday, you'd never asked me to kiss you either. And fuck, I didn't want to wait or distance myself anymore. Not after the way you owned that kiss, owned my fucking mouth."

Holy shit. I was going to explode. Frankie had the power to unravel all thoughts and sense and bring me to my knees while he was at it. He spoke with such passion and certainty that I had no doubt he meant every single word.

"I've changed my mind," I said quickly, breathily, even as I stood and started to strip off my jeans. "The way you've got me worked up, I'm set to detonate. I think we've got time."

Frankie smiled widely as he stood just as fast, tugged off his boxers, tore off my tee, and dragged me back to his room where it was my mission to ride him fast and hard.

CHAPTER EIGHT

FRANKIE

AUSTIN HAD SIDE-EYED ME DURING BREAKFAST, AND while I wasn't ignoring him necessarily, I didn't want to get into anything with him. Not when I only had Ian with me for one more day before he had to leave in the morning. He had another night shift at the hospital.

I did steal Ian away from Jasper, though, promising him I'd return his friend after I'd treated both my guys to lunch.

Jasper's reaction had been sweet, really. He'd grinned so widely he'd looked a little maniacal but had sent us away to pick up Ty with his unspoken blessing. I knew it meant a lot to Ian—and me too, I supposed.

We were picking up Ty from Carter and Tanner's house. It was Carter's mom who'd looked after my boy while also babysitting Libby, Carter and Tanner's niece.

When we arrived in Kirkby and the tree-lined street where their house sat, sound from the back garden reached us. Hand in hand, a connection I found so damn natural and easy, we headed around to the side entrance. I unbolted the wooden gate, and we walked through. Rex, their huge-ass monster of a dog, who was also the sappiest hound I'd ever known, immediately appeared.

He all but slammed into us. I readied myself by protecting my goods. One of these days, I was sure he would headbutt my junk and do permanent damage. Rex managed to stop, though, a bare second before he bowled us over, and proceeded to dance around us, looking for fuss. Their newest puppy, Ralphie, trotted not too far behind Rex. The six-month-old Labrador was ridiculously cute.

Ian scooted low to rub Rex's head affectionately, complete with cooing noises. And when Ralphie nudged in for cuddles, too, Ian swooped in with even more affection. I chuckled at his side, which earned me a quirked brow. But I couldn't not find his puppy-dog speak adorable. He was a built guy, fit as hell, which he'd demonstrated perfectly both last night and then this morning when I'd gone cross-eyed as he'd ridden me good and hard. But it was his stature, which I was sure some found intimidating on first look, that was so at odds with everything else about the man.

He was sweetness personified. While he could say it how it was, and I was sure there was a side to him he used at work that I had yet to see, in every word and gesture he made, he was gentle and caring, and a hell of a lot more considerate than I was.

If I let myself think about just how incredible Ian was, I'd feel like shit, knowing he was too good for me.

But since I'd already ascertained he was a better man than me, I had no desire to tell him as much or let him go. Fuck that. I wanted him as much as I wanted my next breath. I wanted to have all his orgasms, his smiles, and his sweetness.

"Daddy." Ty raced around the corner, Carter behind him, no doubt double-checking who'd arrived.

"Hey, buddy." He charged at me, and I scooped him up into my arms. He planted a big, loud kiss on my lips and hugged the crap out of me. God, I loved this boy so damn much. He was my heart. He eased away after the cuddle, a massive smile on his face. "You had a good time, bud?"

"Yep. Come and push me on the swing." His gaze traveled to Ian, who'd stood from his lovefest with Rex and Ralphie. "Ian, come play. Daddy," he said, looking back at me, "I want Ian to push me."

I snorted. "So that's how it is, huh? Trading me in for a newer model?"

Ty scrunched his nose, clearly having no idea what I meant.

"I'd love to, Ty. Lead the way," Ian said, and I glanced over at him. The gorgeous man's gaze slammed into me, and I saw a slight hesitation there.

We'd never actually gone on to discuss our plans beyond we wanted each other and that we'd try to make it work. There was Ty to consider, absolutely, but it didn't matter that Ian and I had just twenty-four hours of exploring this new shift in our relationship. A year had given me plenty of time to know I wanted him. We were already good friends and knew a lot about each other. Plus, we were phenomenally compatible in bed. And that he was vers but loved to bottom—which I happily discovered this morning—had pretty much cemented the deal for me.

I leaned in and pressed my lips against Ian's. His breath caught, but he angled into the kiss without hesitation. The brief connection I hoped was enough to reassure him there'd be no hiding or even going slow.

Screw that.

When I pulled away, we were both grinning. Ty, however, had a scrunched-up nose.

"What's that face for?" I asked him.

"This is my only face, Daddy," the wiseass said.

I squinted at him and tickled his tummy. "The nose scrunching," I clarified.

"You can only kiss people you married to."

I snorted. "Not true, kiddo. You can only kiss people who you like or love a lot and you want to spend all your time with."

"I likes Libby a lot and don't want kisses with her."

"And you have to be at least twenty-five," I added quickly. Carter's chuckle drew my attention to him. A large grin sat on his face, as though he was thoroughly entertained.

"'Kay," Tyler answered easily, and I smiled in both relief and amusement. This parenting gig was hard as hell, but every moment was beyond incredible. "Ian, you come now."

I coughed lightly.

"Please," Ty quickly added.

"Sure will."

I released my son. Immediately, he grasped Ian's hand and tugged him toward the back of the house and the swing set, leaving me alone with Carter, who watched me intently.

"Looks like you've had an interesting night."

My grin was wide. "I sure have."

He simply bobbed his head, his gaze still assessing, but he didn't question me. A happy squeal filled the air, definitely Tyler's. "Come on. I've just put coffee on. We best go check that Ty and Libby aren't talking Ian into pushing them over the top or something."

I snorted, knowing he spoke the truth. Ty did have a penchant for swinging high and going as fast as possible on his bicycle. The kid was already out of his training wheels too. Last birthday I'd bought him this tiny-ass skateboard, courtesy of him going on and on about wanting to be like my friend Lawrence. I had no issues with that and even picked up one for me to make an ass of myself.

I'd remembered immediately skateboarding was nothing like snowboarding and had a bruise the size of Texas on my ass for a week to prove it.

Together, Carter and I headed out back, where I saw a group of familiar faces. The town had been understandably busy with the festival taking place, and it seemed like quite a few people had congregated here. I knew there were various teams on cleanup duty, but they were from a couple of towns over. Most of the people here, including me, had spent hours setting up, doing our part to get everything up and running. It had been hard work but worth it, even more so as it changed the course of my life.

That kissing booth had undoubtedly proven to be one hell of a success.

"Hey," I greeted everyone and followed up with a cursory glance at Ian, who pushed both kids on the swing set. Ian peered over at me at the same time and threw me a wink. I grinned and then looked away when I accepted my coffee from Marcy, Carter's mom.

"Thanks. Everything been okay?"

Marcy smiled. "Absolutely. He's such a sweet boy."

"He is… when he's not causing chaos," I joked.

"And how about you? A good night?"

I grinned wide. "You could say that."

"It looks like I'm not the only one who could say that either," she responded, looking directly at Ian before casting her gaze back to me.

I chuckled. "News sure does travel fast."

"Well," she said, leaning into me a little, "I may have happened across a certain booth yesterday where I saw some action."

"Well, that'll do it. No secrets when we were in public in the middle of a festival."

"I must admit I was surprised."

My brows dipped, wondering where she was going with this. I'd met the woman a handful of times, liked her a lot, and certainly trusted her enough to care for Ty. But I wasn't quite sure I wanted anyone's opinion about my love life or my sexuality, if that was where she was going.

When I didn't respond, a soft smile appeared. "Don't look so worried. I'm just surprised you'd be okay with Ian having all of that lip action since clearly, you're perfect for each other."

Warmth blossomed in my gut. Not only was I startled by her kind words, but I kinda loved the idea that anyone thought Ian and I were perfect for each other. I couldn't hold back my grin. "You think?" I asked, despite not truly looking for approval. More like enjoying the idea of the support.

"How can I not when the two of you are so handsome and nice. Plus, you should have seen that man's smile when that boy of yours dragged him into the yard. Happy doesn't even begin to describe that look on his face."

"Thanks, Marcy. I appreciate you saying that."

She bobbed her head, adding, "Plus the muscles on the man." Her brows wagged. "I adore Jack, and he's still as handsome today as when I first met him, but there's something about a man who could pick you up and do all manner of things with you.

Something of a caveman fantasy come to life, really."

My laugh was abrupt and loud. "You know, I couldn't agree more," I said, still laughing.

Marcy smirked. "You make the most of it before he hits sixty and his back isn't as strong as it used to be."

My chortle continued. "I absolutely will."

She sighed just as Carter appeared at his mom's side, his brows scrunched.

"Do I want to know?" he asked.

"Caveman fantasies," she said, making Carter blanch and me laugh a little harder.

His nose scrunched. "Pretend I never asked."

"But I would imagine Tanner would do a pretty impressive job. He has quite a few pounds on you, darling boy. His muscles aren't quite like Ian's, but he's got that whole natural strong brawny thing going on. Tell me, Carter, does—"

"Hell no." He shook his head and dashed away like his ass was on fire.

Marcy sighed again. "You know, you'd have thought he'd be used to sharing the details with me now. I've no idea why he gets so uncomfortable."

I could definitely imagine why but didn't want to burst her bubble. I helpfully offered, "Keep at him. I'm sure the more questions you ask, the more at ease he'll be." It was likely I was going to hell, or at least wouldn't get an invite for dinner for a while, but Marcy legit looked forlorn. I couldn't have that.

"You're a good man, Frankie. You be sure to look after that lovely nurse of yours. He's definitely one of the good ones."

I nodded. "I absolutely will."

Jack called her over, and Marcy headed away, leaving me to take everything in.

Ian still pushed both kids. They were all chatting about something, and every now and then, squeals of delight filled the air. What I wouldn't give for this to be my life for real. For somewhere down the line our relationship to have developed to the forever kind of thing, for Tyler to have two parents who loved and supported him.

And here, in this community, it would make it all the more perfect.

But I could go slow since I had no choice in the matter, knowing we'd only be able to catch up a couple of times a month until Ian could find a local job.

The wait would be absolutely worth it.

CHAPTER NINE

IAN

SAYING GOODBYE AND RETURNING TO THE CITY AND TO work had been a struggle.

Every time I left Jasper's place, it was always with a heavy load of reluctance, but this time and for obvious reasons, it was a hundred times more difficult.

But life went on as it was prone to do.

When I worked, ate, and slept, Frankie remained on my mind, even in my dreams. On top of that, we spoke and texted when I had the chance.

Conversation was easy, as it had always been, but throw in phone sex, a complete first for me, and it kept life interesting and made my time pining after the guy a little more bearable.

But still, the past three weeks had not been the great-est, mainly because I worked two weekends in a row, which meant we didn't have the opportunity to see each other.

"That's the fifth time you've got your ass kicked," Jasper said through the headset.

It had been far too long since Jasper and I had got together to do some gaming and simply hang out online. Guilt slithered through me. It had been a while, yet I still wasn't giving him my full attention.

"What's going on?"

"Just tired." While it was the truth, it wasn't the half of it.

"And?"

I released a small snort. He knew me far too well. "I called the hospital at Crescent today."

"And from your glum voice, I'm assuming still no good news?"

"No." I shouldn't have been surprised. For the past year, I'd been trying to get a position. Now a new urgency drove me to want to move.

Long distance sucked. Determination thrummed a steady beat, though. I wanted to make this work with Frankie, more than I'd wanted anything else before. Despite the limited visits, we'd both liked each other for so long that I had no plan for a little thing like a few hundred miles stopping us from seeing this through.

"Did you try the clinics too?"

"Yeah."

"I'm sorry, Ian. I know how much you want this, but it'll give you and Frankie more time to see how things go before it being full-on if you move."

"What's that mean?" I didn't like the punch of tension that kicked in with his words.

"Just that this is so new and it's good not to rush into things, is all."

I pursed my lips, discomfort settling against my skin like a thick blanket on a scorching-hot day. "We've known each other for over two years. Us dancing around each other is hardly rushing things." I didn't manage to keep the full bite from my words.

"Shit, I didn't mean anything bad by it. You're right, I'm sorry. I love Frankie; you too."

"So what, you think us being together isn't a good thing?" The discomfort morphed into dread combined with a swirl of nausea in my gut.

"No, not at all. Seriously, I'm sorry. This is completely me still being surprised by Frankie not being straight, and that's on me. I sound like a dick, and that's not fair on you."

I snorted at his admission, taking in a big breath and relaxing my shoulders a little. "Just stop being a dick, and there's no problem."

He hummed and seemed to hesitate with a clearing of his throat.

"Out with it."

Jasper chuckled. "So, you really didn't know… about Frankie, I mean?"

I shook my head, despite being alone. "Hell no. I could get pretty frustrated about it too."

"You could?"

"All this time we could have been together."

He made a quiet sound, indicating his understanding. "It's sweet."

"What is?"

"The two of you being the way you are, all heart-eyed and besotted."

"Besotted?" Heat hit my cheeks.

"It's a good word."

I rolled my eyes and laughed. "Always an English teacher."

"Always," he answered, a smile in his voice.

Still caught on what he'd said about the two of us, I couldn't help but ask, "So Frankie's all heart-eyed and besotted?" My heart leaped as I said the words, the heat in my cheeks increasing.

"Definitely. I've never seen either of you like this before. You both seem really happy."

"I know I am, and I can only hope Frankie is too."

"Well, from what I can tell, he absolutely is." There was a pause as my thoughts turned to Frankie. An itch crept across my skin, the urge to call him and hear his voice riding me hard. Before I could respond, Jasper's loud, exaggerated sigh filtered through the headset. "Be gone. Go and call the guy.

Hell, I'm surprised he hasn't invaded the house already, as he knows we're hanging out. He had this whole sulky look on his face earlier. Feel free to tease him about it."

I grinned widely. "Thanks, Jasper. You're the best. I may just do that."

"Good, but when you're next here, carve at least a little time for me, okay?"

"Absolutely."

"Chat soon then."

After I said goodbye, I shut down my Xbox, pulled off my headset, and picked up my cell. Tyler should be asleep by now, so it should be a good time to call.

Disappointment shot to the surface when it went straight to voicemail. I assumed his phone was dead, which sucked. The call would have to wait till tomorrow.

FOR THE PAST NINE HOURS, I'D BEEN RUSHED OFF MY feet. While it was the norm, it seemed like there'd been no short supply of idiotic patients around. The number of them who stumbled in from doing the dumbest stuff never ceased to amaze me. I was just finishing off my notes on a patient who looked like Veruca Salt—post-blueberry incident—who'd gone a few rounds with Tyson Fury, when Helen stepped to my side, letting me know my boyfriend was here waiting to see me.

"My boyfriend?" My heart flipped over, worry and excitement battling it out, wondering why Frankie was here and latching on to the idea he'd called himself my boyfriend.

"He's fine. Calm your jets," she said with a smirk. "No injuries. When I heard him asking for you, I shuffled him into room five." She followed up with a wink, and relief made my heart flutter. That he was okay meant I could breathe easier. But that he was here? I shook my head, knowing the only way to find that out was to go and see the guy.

I quickly called out to Janice, letting her know I needed fifteen minutes, and asked her to check on the patient in twelve.

Once she agreed, I hurried in the direction of five, my stomach running amok and making basic things like remembering to breathe difficult. I also pulled out my phone from my pants pocket. There were no new messages from Frankie.

I tugged back the curtain wearing a giant smile. It fell instantly.

Leroy.

"Hey." He stood from the chair and grinned. "You look great."

My brows scrunched together, and I placed my cell on the small counter at the entrance. The guy looked honest-to-God happy to see me. I was tempted to glance around the room searching for hidden cameras, but with the eerily large smile on his face, there was no chance I'd take my eyes off him.

"Leroy?" I shook my head, still frowning. "What are you doing here?"

His smile faltered, but only for a second before it stretched fully, almost maniacally. "I thought you needed a little time to calm down and get whatever happened in that little hick town out of your system. You get off in ten minutes, right? So I thought we could grab dinner."

Unease slammed into me, thick and fast. I swore I was a magnet for obsessive psychos. "I'm not off for a while," I answered, with no idea how he knew my shift was ending. Not only that, I hadn't a clue how to respond to the guy short of calling security and telling him to back off. But drama of any sort, especially at work, wasn't on my to-do list on any given day.

His grin shifted to a smirk, and he tilted his head. "Playing coy is all levels of sexy. I can wait outside for you if you don't want the staff to know I'm picking you up for a date."

My brows raised high, and I stared at him in disbelief, especially since he'd already declared himself as my boyfriend. The last thing I wanted to do was engage the guy in conversation, question what the hell planet he'd escaped from. I sighed in defeat. Perhaps calling security was the only way to go. "I need you to leave."

Leroy bobbed his head, his tall, slim frame too close for my comfort. "I can do that. Out the front okay?"

"No," I said, shaking my head. "Of course it's not okay. We're not going on a date. I don't even know why you think it would be okay that you're here."

He pouted, looking ridiculous. "But ever since that night, I knew we had that spark, that something special."

I was shaking my head before he even finished. "No, you're delusional. You need to leave."

When his jaw tightened, I tensed. There was a security alarm on the wall just behind me. It would be mortifying to touch the damn thing, but I would if I had to.

"You really don't want dinner?"

"I really don't."

Leroy pursed his lips, gaze assessing. I held back my sneer, hating his eyes on me.

"Fine, I'll go if you'll give me that kiss you owe me."

I scoffed. "Not happening."

He hesitated. "How about a goodbye hug?"

This man was seriously unhinged. "Nope."

"Just a brief hug, and then I promise not to come back here ever again... unless you want me to."

My hesitation was a mistake. Leroy caught onto it immediately. "Honestly, a goodbye hug between friends, then I'm out of here. See it as an apology for me overstepping." Wide-eyed, he peered at me, his palms open as he spoke.

I was a fool, but a two-second hug and him disappearing for good would save a whole lot of drama and paperwork. "Fine, but I'm serious. That's it. No waiting for me, no asking me on a date. I have a boyfriend."

A flicker of something registered in his eyes, but it cleared quickly as he stepped toward me. "Scout's honor." The next step, Leroy wrapped his arms around me, and I stood rigid, wondering what the fuck I was doing, letting this creep touch me.

But then it was over. There was no trying for a feel, no weird sniffing, no overlong hug. I exhaled in relief and turned to watch Leroy leave as he stepped around me.

He threw me a smile and a wink over his shoulder, and I barely contained my shudder as he disappeared from my sight. I hoped for good.

Frazzled and annoyed by the whole strange last five minutes of my life, the first thing I did was wash my hands. I felt dirty and a little uneasy. After that, I finished off the chart I was working on and, thirty minutes later, hesitated at the main entrance, hoping Leroy wasn't waiting for me.

I took a deep breath and headed to my car, pleased it was still light outside. Once safely in my seat and the engine running, I exhaled and stretched some of the tension away from my neck.

I needed a beer, a hot shower, and to hear Frankie's voice. It was the thought of the latter that had me smiling as I pulled out of the parking space.

CHAPTER TEN

FRANKIE

I'D MISSED IAN'S CALL A COUPLE OF NIGHTS AGO, AND last night my own calls went unanswered. The same tonight. A sliver of worry crept into my thoughts, first wondering if everything was okay and then hoping he wasn't annoyed with me and ignoring my calls deliberately. As soon as the latter thought entered my mind, I dismissed it. Ian wasn't a man who played games. Well, I thought with a private smirk, he was open to some games of the sexy variety on video call, but that was about it.

"You heard from Ian?" I asked Jasper. He was at the kitchen table marking some papers. I'd invited myself around to grill him about his best friend.

"Hello to you too," he said with a quirked brow.

I grinned in response. "Hey, Jasper, good day? Great. You heard from Ian?"

Jasper's response was to snort out a laugh and roll his eyes. "Yes, I've had a great day. Thanks for asking. And no, I haven't heard from Ian since our game a couple of nights ago." His smile slipped. "Why? There's not a problem, is there?"

As I huffed out a somewhat pathetic sigh, I sat at the table, casting a quick look at Ty. He was happily emptying the box of toys that he kept here. I returned my focus to Jasper, whose brows were creased, worry etched in his features.

"No, I don't think so. We've just been playing phone tag, but Ian hasn't returned my texts either."

Jasper's frown became more pronounced. "I texted him last night, and he didn't answer. I assumed he'd had an early night, is all. I'm sure it's nothing to worry about."

My answering hum called bullshit, especially as Jasper's expression mirrored my own.

"Do you know if he's working today?"

I nodded. "Yeah, his shift starts in a couple of hours."

Jasper's shoulders relaxed marginally. "He's no doubt just sleeping in. He'll call later, I'm sure. What are you getting into today?"

"Not much. Ty and I are having a lazy day. If the rain stays away, we'll probably head to the park this afternoon."

"Cool. If you do and want company, let me know. That brother of yours has to work in the office all day."

I scrunched my nose up. "He works too damn hard."

"He sure does. But doing it now means he should be home all next week at a decent time, so it's all good. Nature of the beast, I suppose."

He was right. It also reaffirmed why I wasn't cut out to be a teacher, let alone in admin as a principal. Hell to the no. An office job was already proving a huge change compared to my more carefree days of following seasons and the snow. I glanced over at Ty and smiled as he played with a T. rex, a Barbie, and an assortment of cars. My boy was worth it all, though, and staying put and making a new life for myself, having my own family, was hardly a sacrifice.

I'd had years of bumming around and had loved every moment, but this, having Ty, was so much better.

But it would be even better if I could get in touch with Ian.

The man was constantly on my mind. While we'd only had one official weekend together, we'd talked daily. It already seemed like so much longer. Though I supposed that was what over a year of friendship did to a relationship. I had no doubt that's what this thing was between us. A full-on, grown-up relationship. And fuck if I wasn't excited about the prospect of spending as much time with the man as possible, not only by ourselves but with Ty too.

"Company at the park would be good if you and Penny want to come with," I finally said, pulling out my phone.

"You going to try again?" Jasper asked, nodding toward the cell.

"Yeah. I'll shoot Ian a text, just so he gets it when he wakes up, so he doesn't panic."

Jasper threw me a smile. "Good idea. A bunch of missed calls and he'll worry, thinking something's wrong."

Perhaps I should have been embarrassed when I said, "I'm coming across pretty needy, huh?" But I didn't have it in me. I was needy, dammit, and had no issues with who knew how important Ian was to me.

A shrug accompanied Jasper's words. "It's sweet."

I smiled. "Who knew I had it in me, right?"

"Ha! I wouldn't go that far, but it is all levels of adorable. I'm pleased things are working out for you."

My heart flipped at his words, and I agreed whole-heartedly. I was beyond happy things were working out between Ian and me too.

"Thanks, Jasper." I winked before turning my attention to my phone.

Me: Hope everything's okay and you're managing decent sleep. Call me when you're awake. Nothing's wrong my end. Just miss your voice.

Just as I was closing my phone, three dancing dots appeared. I expelled a rush of air and smiled. The sound must have been noisy, since Jasper looked over. "He answered?"

"About to," I said, grinning.

He shot me a smile and returned to his work while I focused on the incoming text.

Ian: Everything has been happening so fast and we made a mistake. We need to hit pause. Don't make this more difficult. Don't contact me.

"What the fuck?" My stomach hollowed out, and my gaze shot up to meet Jasper's concerned one.

"What's wrong?"

"The hell if I know, but this is bullshit."

I hit Call without another thought—my single aim to speak to Ian and find out what was going on. The text, him not contacting me, none of this was like him at all.

Immediately the call went to voicemail. Ian's sexy voice told me to leave a message, but there was no way I could do that.

"Frankie?"

The worry in Jasper's voice had me snapping my attention back to him. Without speaking, I thrust the phone at him and shook my head.

I could tell when the words in the text registered. Jasper's brows shot high, and his focus returned to me.

"This—" Jasper hesitated.

"Right!" I cut in. He didn't need to finish for us both to know that something was off.

As he passed me back my cell, his hand was already in his pocket. Phone in hand, he scrolled through and hit a button, the phone going to his ear. "Voicemail."

My ass hit the wooden seat of the chair hard. With my mind whirling and my heart racing at the weirdness of the text and the shock of the words, I struggled to get my thoughts together.

"Ian said anything to you, indicated there's a problem?" Even as I asked the question, I knew the answer was no in my gut. Jasper's shake of his head simply confirmed it.

A quick glance at my boy, who was so innocently unaware as he played with his toys, and a flicker of certainty flared to life in my chest. Something wasn't right. While that seemed obvious considering the text I'd received, my concern bled deeper. For Ian to send me a text like that was out of character. I was fully aware we'd spent virtually no time together since becoming a couple, but still, I knew how I felt. And considering how well I thought I knew Ian, I didn't hesitate to believe that he felt the same way.

"So—"

Jasper didn't give me the chance to finish my thought. "I'll happily look after Ty, and if you're not back tonight, I'll be sure he's well taken care of tomorrow."

I grinned and stood, reaching out and squeezing his shoulder. "Thanks, man."

"Anytime. Just go and sort this out, check Ian's okay." The worry reflected in his eyes was easy to read.

"On it."

Thirty minutes later, after cuddles and kisses with Ty and promises that he could speak to me anytime he wanted or needed, I was on the road. I expected by the time I got there, Ian would be at work. All the easier to track him down and find out what the hell was happening.

CHAPTER ELEVEN

IAN

HARASSED DIDN'T EVEN COME CLOSE TO DESCRIBING how I felt. Somehow I'd lost my phone, and because I was barely functioning on a few hours' sleep, I hadn't had the time or energy to report it as lost. I'd checked my bill online again as soon as I'd woken, and no calls or texts had been made, which was something. But between yesterday's unplanned four-teen-hour shift and this morning me waking up late, giving me only thirty minutes to get my ass into gear, I was stressed.

That and, of course, the fact I'd yet to memorize anyone's number meant that I dreaded to think what was going through Frankie's mind.

"Who pissed in your cereal?"

I cast a sharp look at Gerald, one of the orderlies. His brows shot high, and he took a step back.

"Whoa, easy there, tiger."

I sighed. "Sorry. Just had a couple of days of it."

"Anything I can do?"

Gerald's words pulled a reluctant smile from me. He was a good guy who regularly went above and beyond for me.

"I can't find my phone."

"Again?" Immediately his hands lifted as though to ward me off. It was rare I was this agitated, but when I was, those who knew me well were aware to look out. "Uhm, what I meant to say was have you used that phone finder app to look at its last location?"

I hadn't, which made me feel idiotic, especially since I'd been online to check my calls with the billing company. "No," I admitted, rolling my eyes at myself. "That would take common sense, which I'm on short supply of when I'm running on limited sleep and a whole lot of pissed off."

"What are you meant to be doing now, and is it something I can do so you can jump on a computer to check?"

The tension sitting heavily on my shoulders eased, and my smile this time was wide. "You're too good to me. You sure?"

Gerald nodded. "Course. I owe you a few good deeds, the number of times you've had my back."

After five minutes of explaining to him the few admin tasks I could get away with him doing since they didn't need a nurse, I patted him on the back and raced off to find an unoccupied computer.

It didn't take long to log into my account and click on my phone to track its location. Confusion burrowed deep inside. My brows dropped low, and my stomach flipped a little.

My cell's last location was a couple of hours ago and about three hours from here. Not anywhere I'd been. "Shit." I should have just canceled my phone. Some asswipe had managed to steal the damn thing. With a sigh, I activated the Mark as Lost option.

I knew the procedure well, but never with my phone clearly being full-on stolen before. In the past, I'd left it in a club and even in the pediatrics department. While I'd have to call Apple and make a claim, I didn't have the time right this moment. But at least with the lost mode being activated, my phone would be locked and my account safe.

Frustrated I'd left it so long, I checked the time on the wall clock. I could probably get away with ten more minutes.

I quickly opened Instagram, planning to message Frankie, though not actually sure I could send a message from a PC rather than a phone. It was no good anyway. "For shit's sake." I shook my head at the site and its security, telling me it would send me a text to verify it was me. "Really freakin' useful."

"Not good then, huh?" Gerald's voice pulled my attention away from social media and their ridiculous security measure. Sure, I knew it was a good thing, but not when I was trying to get a message out to Frankie.

"No. Some thieving ass stole it."

Gerald grimaced. "Sucks, man. You blocked it?"

"Yeah. I'll deal with a new phone and everything else later." A new sigh escaped, this one intending to get rid of the negativity blanketing me. I forced a smile. "Thanks for covering for me. Everything okay?"

"No problems at all. Just letting you know Dr. Basil is looking for you."

"Okay, thanks again. I best go and see what she's after."

Gerald left the office space with a small wave, leaving me to get myself back together. Finding Basil when I was so agitated wouldn't go down great. She could be officious, and she certainly had no time for anyone with a bad attitude.

I headed out to the nurses' station with no other choice, needing to pick up some charts en route to finding Basil. I still had hours to go before the end of my shift, so getting stuck in and getting over myself was the easiest thing to do.

"I BEST GO AND CHANGE." I WRINKLED MY NOSE AT THE substance covering my scrubs. There was no way I'd think too hard about what stained me. It wouldn't do my headspace any good, since I was already ruffled.

Karen snickered when she realized what covered me. "Yeah, you best. I'll finish up here."

I nodded my thanks and bolted. Funnily, I made it to the staff shower without being accosted once. Hell, maybe I should have thrown crap on myself more often. It was a simple, though totally gross, way to keep the hordes of staff away from me.

Just as I opened the shower door, Gerald called out to me. "Who's the hottie asking for you in the waiting area?"

I turned to look at Gerald, giving a full view of my condition. Nose scrunching, he stepped back.

"Uhm, I'll tell them you'll need a few minutes."

"What? Who's here?" I was too tired for any more shit today. Literally.

Gerald shrugged. "Uhm, something about your boyfriend?"

I understood his hesitancy, especially as I was sure he saw the white-hot anger morph onto my face as it raced through my veins.

"Ian, you okay, man?"

Uncertainty danced on his features. I tried to rein in my anger. How I was behaving was so not me, and I could probably count on one hand how many times in all my years of nursing anyone had seen me lose my cool. And in this fairly new job, it was a lot less than five digits.

The word "boyfriend" bounced around in my head. That *fucker*. Somehow I contained my words, not wanting to let go and make this day any worse. But if Leroy continued to think he could do this... mess with me, especially when I was at work, he had another think coming.

My patience was officially gone. Torn at the seams, broken down into the tiniest of threads.

"Out front?" I asked through clenched teeth.

Gerald nodded. "Uhm... clothes?" He eyed my scrubs, and the reminder made me falter. I was tempted to head out anyway, but then the stench hit me, and I thought better.

I grunted in response, turned, headed to my locker for fresh scrubs, then washed myself down in the shower.

As I cleaned, I focused on calming myself. It wouldn't do me any good to race out guns blazing. Plus, that would only piss my superiors off. This time though, I had no second thoughts about contacting security should I need to.

I toweled off and dressed, wondering why so many dickheads felt the need to display such obsessive behavior toward me. When I'd met Scott and Davis a few years back in a club, as a loved-up couple, I'd felt gut-deep they were safe. Completely over being harassed by a guy who wouldn't leave me alone, I'd selected them as my safe haven. It was because of them I'd met Jasper, whose friendship kept me sane. And because of him, I had Frankie in my life.

Just the thought of the man who turned my world upside down in the best of ways slowed down my racing heart. I shook out my fingers and loosened my neck muscles. I had to believe everything happened for a reason, believe that events had a way of connecting and leading me to the good stuff.

With that in mind and thoughts of Frankie swirling in my head, I smiled.

Leroy was insignificant, and whatever he was playing at, I'd shut it down today. Complications and negativity were not welcome in my life.

I headed out of the staff locker room and toward the main waiting area with a sure step. The next few minutes were likely going to be unpleasant, but I could cope with a little trouble to ensure a whole lot of the happy stuff.

I stopped short when I gazed around the area, my eyes widening in surprise. "Frankie."

Before I could react any more, he was on his feet and traveling in my direction. Worry filled his eyes, an expression I hadn't seen on him before, or certainly not to this extreme.

Once before me, he hesitated, hand moving as though to reach out to me before he pulled it back.

I crinkled my brows, not only concerned by his presence but also that he didn't greet me how he appeared to want to. Frankie wasn't a man affected by others' thoughts and opinions, so I was confident it wasn't that.

"You okay?" Doubt bled through my words. How could they not? While my heart beat faster with the surprise visit and I wanted nothing more than to lean into him and capture his lips, the uncertainty surrounding us pressed hard on my chest.

"You have a few minutes?"

I nodded, hating the dread pounding through me. I led Frankie down a corridor and to an empty room. Once inside, I closed the door, unsure if I should smile, hug him, or puke.

"What's wrong?"

Frankie scrunched his brows together in response to my question. "That's what I was here to ask you. I don't understand what's going on. What's changed?"

Bewildered, I shook my head. I pulled apart my thoughts, trying to understand his words. Was this because it had been a few days since we'd spoken to each other? If that was the case, it was kinda sweet he'd come all this way to talk to me, but a bit odd too. I swallowed hard at the next word that popped into my head. *Obsessive*. I shook my head. That couldn't be it. Nothing about Frankie screamed obsessive behavior.

"Is this about us not speaking?" I needed clarity. My chest tightened in anticipation, my mind searching for answers I hoped would come soon.

"Your text," he said, taking a step toward me but not reaching out—the fact he didn't sent with it a new wave of confusion. We hadn't seen each other in a while. The whole time, literally every day of us not being together, I'd imagined our next moment together. The version going on right now was nothing like I'd imagined—me pouncing on him, hauling him up, and getting wrapped up in him.

My brows scrunched, his words finally registering. "Text?" I thought back to the last texts we'd exchanged before I'd lost—no, that was no longer accurate—before my phone had been stolen. Nothing came to mind. "What text? When?"

"A few hours ago. You sent—"

"I haven't had my phone for a couple of days," I rushed to say, cutting him off, my brain working overdrive, bewildered.

"What do you mean?" Frankie tucked his hands in his jeans pockets, looking puzzled.

"I thought I'd misplaced it. I found out it's been stolen. Only blocked it a couple of hours ago, though."

While Frankie was already looking at me, at my words, his gaze sharpened. "It was stolen?"

I nodded and grunted hard when Frankie all but slammed into me, enveloping me in a hug. His lips found purchase on my neck, a light kiss settling there before he angled away, breathing the words, "Thank Christ." The brilliant smile I loved was directed at me. "Shit, Ian. I raced on over here ready to throw you over my shoulder and kidnap you to talk some sense into you."

His infectious laughter followed, impossible to ignore and not join in with.

"I still have no clue what you're talking about." While happy he was before me, and he seemed super pleased my phone had been stolen, I needed to understand what was going on. Fully aware I was at work and there wasn't a chance I could sneak away for much longer, I needed answers.

My gaze followed his hand to his pocket. He tugged out his phone, unlocked it, searched for something, and passed it to me. I took his cell with a frown.

A heaviness settled in the pit of my stomach when I read the text coming from my number. I jerked my head back and made eye contact with Frankie, who watched my every reaction.

"That wasn't me. I didn't send that."

Frankie's gaze searched my own before he expelled a loud breath. "Thank Christ for that," he said, his hands immediately on my forearms and tugging me close to him. I went willingly, enjoying the contact and the comfort of his embrace. "I knew something wasn't right. It's why I jumped in the car straight-away to come see you." His warm breath brushed across my neck. Goose bumps erupted, and a delightful shiver worked its way through my limbs.

That Frankie had immediately come to me, asked questions, wanted clarity rather than taking the false words as gospel meant everything. I wanted to stay like this, bask in this moment. Frankie cared, a lot, and I was more than okay with that.

There was a lot to figure out, not only with my missing cell and the text that could have cost me my chance with the incredible man still pressed close to me but also with how we could make this work for real. Spending so much time apart was a serious pain in the ass.

It didn't matter that I was certain we could do long-distance for as long as needed. The bottom line was I didn't want to see Frankie sporadically.

"Ian." My name was followed by two loud raps on the door. It didn't surprise me that I'd been spotted coming in here.

I pulled away from Frankie and called out, "Yeah?"

"You're needed in room six."

"Coming."

Turning my attention back to Frankie, I swept the pad of my thumb across his cheek. "Thank you for coming. It means a lot."

Frankie's crooked grin was sexy at the best of times, but with emotions swirling in his eyes, he'd never looked so handsome. "I'll always chase you, Ian."

I beamed at his words, basking in the glow of the moment.

"I have no plans to let you go."

Ever, I thought, hoping we were on the same page.

"Can you stay? Tonight?" I clarified. Tyler would be well looked after, I was sure of it. There wasn't a chance Frankie would be here without him if not.

"I think that can be arranged."

The temptation was too great. I brushed my lips against his, opening slightly, just enough for one sweep of my tongue over his bottom lip. "Let me grab you my key. I've still got a few hours, but I'll be back as soon as possible. You've got the address?"

"Yeah, and sounds good." Frankie captured my mouth once more before I could pull away, and I melted against him, savoring his taste and touch. All too soon, he eased away. It was a good job one of us was thinking clearly. I could have easily barricaded us into the small office and spread myself out for him on the desk.

"Whatever you're thinking, save it till you get home." He squeezed my ass cheek for good measure, and I grunted, flexing my glutes before turning and grinning when Frankie groaned, mumbling, "Tonight, your ass is mine."

I had no problems with that at all.

CHAPTER TWELVE

THE WHOLE DRIVE TO SEE IAN, MY MIND HAD GONE TO the worst-case scenario: that maybe he'd meant the words and we were really over. Now, as I poured a glass of wine before settling in front of Ian's Xbox, those few hours already seemed like a distant nightmare.

Something had been off with the text. I'd known it gut-deep. My relief at the hospital learning Ian's phone had been stolen had been downright palpable. The urge to not let Ian go rode me hard. That hadn't changed since we'd shared our first kiss, and he'd shown he was absolutely as into me as I was him.

It was a heady feeling, finally having Ian as mine. The past few weeks had been a whirlwind of kisses and calls and counting the hours till we could see each other again. Seriously, long-distance sucked spectacularly, but after a year of waiting and being without Ian's kisses, without his affection, I could wait as long as it took for us to be able to see each other every damn day.

I looked at the screen, smirking when I saw Jasper's gamer handle accept my invite. Once I'd found Ian's headphones and placed them on, I'd opened up a random game and invited Jasper.

"Hey," I said into the mic.

"Frankie?"

I laughed. "Yeah. Ian's still at work."

"I thought it was too early for him."

"How's Ty?"

"Fast asleep. He settled easily."

Warmth filled my chest thinking about my sweet boy and how much he was loved, not only by me, but my whole family. Jasper, my almost brother-in-law, and Ian were definitely included in that group.

"Thanks again for looking after him last minute."

"No worries. I'm just relieved you figured everything out. Did Ian say anything about who could have texted?"

"Nothing. We didn't really get time to talk." But it was something we absolutely needed to discuss and figure out. That his phone had been stolen was a given, and honestly, not that uncommon. But that whoever the culprit was didn't just reset the phone, or whatever, which I assumed was possible, and instead responded to my message with something so specific and set to hurt was suspicious as hell.

Who the fuck would do something like that?

I hoped to God we found out, because that shit, messing with me and Ian like that, was sick.

"It's weird, though, right?"

"It sure is." I huffed out a sigh, feeling tense once again thinking about this whole phone debacle.

"You need me to kick your ass at something?" Humor laced his voice. Jasper was a good guy. Not only did he make my brother disgustingly happy, but he knew when I needed a distraction.

I snorted. "Sure. Just don't go tattle-taleing to that brother of mine when you lose spectacularly."

"Ha. Just get the Kleenex handy for when you cry all the tears when I defeat you."

Laughter bubbled out of me as we got stuck into a racing game. From the onset, it was clear Jasper spent far too long gaming.

"Dude, for real, do you have any other hobbies?" Jasper didn't merely kick my ass. He annihilated me. Full-on destroyed me. Every. Single. Time.

"Gaming, teaching, or going down on your broth—"

"Hell no!"

He laughed loud and hard when I cut him off.

"Say another word and I'm going to have to, like scrub my ears or something." Jasper's laughter continued as I shrieked a loud "Fuck!" I wrenched off the headset to see a wide-eyed Ian angled toward me. "Holy fuck. I nearly shit myself."

"Easy there. I've dealt with more than enough excrement today, enough for more than one lifetime."

"I'm not going to ask."

"Please don't. And the screaming? You don't want my lips on you?" Ian raised his brows at me.

I grinned and stood, my heart still beating like crazy. I pressed a hand to my chest and smiled even wider when Ian's large hand pressed against mine. "You can place your lips anywhere and whenever you like."

Ian smirked and leaned closer.

"Frankie!"

I winced, pulling back before Ian's mouth made contact. "That'll be Jasper." His loud screech of my name sounded again, and I quickly put the head-phones back on. "I'm here."

"Jesus. You about gave me heart failure."

I snorted. "You and me both. Ian's home." My gaze connected with Ian's as I spoke. I took a moment to get a good look at the man before me. He was still in scrubs and filled out every inch of the fabric to perfection. The guy worked out a fair amount and was just the right side of muscled perfection. He still had a gorgeous neck—his shoulders nowhere near so big that it hindered me licking along the long length of it, which I planned to do as soon as I switched off the Xbox.

Jasper's quiet laughter returned my attention to him. "And clearly, you're already distracted. Go on and spend some time together. Give me a call or text tomorrow when you're leaving, okay?"

"Absolutely. Thanks, Jasper. Speak tomorrow."

"Bye, Jasper," Ian called out.

"See you, Ian."

That was my cue to disconnect and give my full attention to the incredible man before me.

"You want to try that kiss again?"

He grinned as he stepped into my space, his hands moving to cup my face, which I loved. In all my years, I'd never been close enough to have this connection or sweetness with anyone before. And Ian had sweetness and a whole lot of sugar-coated goodness in him.

I was eager to lick him right up and get my Ian fix.

"I missed you." His intense gaze met mine when he spoke.

"Missed you too."

He captured my mouth, stealing my breath. I was lost in the man. My senses in overdrive, I absorbed every touch, groan, and flurry of heat passing between us. With our tongues touching, mouths moving, a spiral of desire burst free, right along with a needy groan.

An honest-to-God whimper escaped when he pulled his mouth away. I clutched him close, not wanting him to move an inch. His whispered words caught my attention, though, stopping me from dragging his mouth back to mine.

"Bedroom."

I nodded, held his hand, eagerly leading the way. I'd previously had a look around, not at all ashamed to have found condoms and a bottle of lube, which proudly sat on his bedside table.

He grinned when he spotted them. "Been busy while you were waiting?"

"You have no idea," I said, tugging off his clothes before redirecting my energy to stripping naked when he worked on kicking off his running shoes.

"I showered at work before I left." The words were said pressed against my throat. Light kisses followed their wake. "Wanted to get myself ready for you, knew it would be impossible to wait as soon as I saw you."

I groaned and tugged his mouth back to mine, loving he knew how hard I'd be for him. "On your hands and knees," I said with a heavy breath, needing him with a fierceness I'd never experienced before.

A smile stretched his face, and he all but leaped onto the bed, getting himself ready for me. I was on him immediately, working him open, licking and tracing his skin, gripping his cock, building him up to the same level of frenzy racing through my veins.

"I'm ready. Just want you." The need in his voice had me reaching for a condom and lubricating thoroughly. His ass would feel so good that I could already imagine his grip and heat. "Frankie, baby, come on."

I leaned over, encouraging Ian to angle for a kiss. He moved willingly, his tongue tangling with mine before I pulled away, positioned myself, and entered him. It was slow going and perfect. Each moan breaking free from him as he gasped at the intrusion, small noises escaping as he pleaded for more, threatened to undo me.

When he begged, there was no holding back.

Warmth swept through every inch of me as Ian gripped me hard, and as we moved, his whimpers soon turning to cries of ecstasy, I angled to tap him hard and fast. I needed him over the edge, needed him to call out my name, and above all else, I needed him to promise to only be mine.

My name spilled from his mouth as I took hold of his cock. Draped over him, my hips still moving, my hand trying to find the perfect rhythm to blow his mind, I didn't have to wait long. Once more, my name escaped him. This time the word was raspy, deep, guttural.

"Fuck." I closed my eyes as the word shot out, right with me emptying inside him. I jerked and twitched, managed a few gentle strokes, massaging his release over his cock.

Without warning, he dropped his arms, head going to the mattress. I grunted and laughed as I fell with him, groaning when his ass clamped down on my sensitive dick. "Warn a guy." I kissed his back, still smiling.

"Sorry. Dead."

I snorted. "No dying on me." I kissed his damp skin once more before pulling away. "Let me clean up. Wait here."

"You sure?"

"I'm positive."

The exhaustion in Ian's voice was loud and clear. I wouldn't have been surprised if he was asleep by the time I cleaned him up. I'd love to let him drift off, but the man needed to eat first.

With a warm washcloth, I wiped his back and gorgeous ass, forcing him to turn over for me. His grunt was sleepy and unimpressed.

"Let me clean you and feed you. Then you can rest, okay?"

Ian peeked open an eye at my words, and a slow smile formed. "I could get used to you looking after me like this."

A flutter came to life in my heart. With his messy sex-mussed hair and sleepy smile, this was quite possibly my favorite look on Ian. And the gentle way he spoke, the way he couldn't quite believe I was taking care of him, made it hard to not hold him close and promise forever.

I wanted us to get to that point. Determination for that to happen one day sparked to life in my chest. "Looking after you is one of my new favorite things to do." I punctuated my words with a kiss before wiping him down and encouraging him to get up so we could eat.

It didn't take long for us to eat and sit back on his couch, letting our food go down.

"Thanks for cooking. I can't believe I didn't smell the food when I came home."

"Your attention may have been focused elsewhere."

"True. But keep cooking like that and greeting me at the door by tearing my clothes off, and I may find it hard to let you go." His words turned shy as he finished speaking.

I squeezed his hand lightly. "Us being so far apart won't be forever."

He bobbed his head, his gaze turning more serious. "So, me moving... I know it was always the plan before this." Ian indicated between us, and I raised my brows.

"'This' as in when we became a couple? Before we started our relationship?"

Pink traveled across his cheeks and a smile quickly followed. "Yes, before we got together, so even though it was always my intention, you're fully on board with me close, right?"

While we'd dipped into this conversation before, perhaps I needed to spell it out for him. "I want you close by so we can give this relationship a chance. I cared about you a long time before you accosted me at the festival." I snorted at his raised brow.

"That's not quite how I remember it."

"No?"

"No. More like the only way you could get these lips on you was by paying me." He laughed loudly, and I reached out and caressed his bare thigh, super close to the bulge covered by the soft fabric of his sleep shorts.

"Is that what happened?"

Narrow eyes peered back at me, and the bulge in his shorts moved and bobbed, creating a growing tent. "How about we figure out a story together?"

I grinned. "We can totally do that as long as it highlights how heroic I was taking one for the team and saving the day." My words didn't get the laughter I expected. Instead, Ian's brows furrowed, his gaze zoning out a little. "Hey, what is it?"

The shake of his head preceded one word: "Leroy."

My hackles raised at the mention of the dickwad's name. "What about him?"

"He came to the hospital a couple of days ago."

My breath stuttered as a lead weight formed and pressed against me. "What happened?" Tension sparked to life, filling my limbs and teasing the edges of my vision at the growing anger knowing Leroy hadn't backed off.

"He got in saying he was my boyfriend." Ian winced, probably a lot to do with my spark of anger lighting up loud and fierce, threatening to turn into wildfire.

"The fuck?"

Ian shook his head. "He came onto me. I shut him down, and he finally left, promising not to come back." Pressing his lips together, he shook his head again. "I think he stole my phone."

THE NEXT COUPLE OF HOURS CONSISTED OF SO MANY phone calls, my head buzzed. But my anger simmered so that my hands no longer shook. There was a moment where Ian had to talk me out of jumping in my car and rocking up at Leroy's house. I had no doubt I'd be able to find his address with just a couple of calls should I need to.

Billy, a guy who worked a few hours a week for my brother, was a former cop with friends still in the police force. I was more than prepared to pull in a favor. I'd already spoken to him, asking about restraining orders. He'd pointed me in the right direction for Ian to file for a protective order, and in the morning before Ian headed to work and I left for home, our first stop would be the local police station.

Ian had called his boss and arranged an appointment with HR in the morning. Calls were also made to the phone company, and we went online and printed out the screenshot of the last known address of the phone. I wasn't sure if the location was Leroy's place or not, but I really hoped it was. Any evidence we could stack against the guy so a restraining order would stick, all the better.

"Please stop and come to bed."

I glanced away from my phone and looked at Ian. Fatigue clouded his features, reminding me that while I was angry, I had no idea how he was feeling or coping. "Okay." I took his offered hand, and we headed to his bedroom. In no time at all, I curved around him, taking refuge in his large arms.

"You okay?" I asked.

The sigh lifted my head up before settling back down from where it was positioned on his chest. "Yeah. I just hoped to avoid all this, you know?"

Even though it was the last thing I wanted him to do, I knew I needed to make it clear he had choices. "If you don't want to make a report and then file for a protective order, you don't have to."

Ian remained quiet for a beat, his soft breathing the only sound in the room. I heard him swallow before saying, "Do you think I should?"

"I know I should say the right thing and let you know it's not about what I want, but this guy tried to screw with you, with us." I closed my eyes to ease my racing heart. "Do I think you're at risk and he's going to be violent or something? I don't know. I suppose I don't think so, but what he's been doing isn't okay. Will he stop and move on by himself?" I shrugged. "Again, I don't know, but if you think it's likely he won't, if you're concerned he's going to carry on and you're spending time worrying, then all of that needs to influence your decision."

Despite the seriousness of our conversation, he chuckled. "So that's a yes then?"

I grunted out a laugh. "That obvious, huh?"

"Just a little." A kiss on the top of my head followed, and I sighed, content in his arms.

"I'll go to the police tomorrow and then look at what's needed for a protective order. Maybe simply knowing that will make him back off for good."

"Sounds good." I yawned. "You tired enough to sleep?" I asked. It was getting late, and after the stress of today, exhaustion bit at my heels.

"I'm surprised I'm still coherent." Ian yawned, the sound almost like a squeak. I snorted. "Hey, leave my yawn alone. It's adorable."

"Yeah, who said that?"

"You did about seven months ago."

My heart lightened at his words, a happy glow filling my soul that he would remember such a thing. I angled up to see his face. The corners of his mouth tilted upwards in a sleepy smile. "It is adorable." Pressing my lips against his, I smiled a little and pulled away. "Let's get some sleep, and we'll get everything fixed up tomorrow."

Ian nodded, and I returned my head to his chest, realizing snuggling with him needed to be added to my absolute favorite things to do.

CHAPTER THIRTEEN

IAN

NERVES DANCED A WILD BEAT IN MY STOMACH. I'D waited for this opportunity for so long, I still couldn't quite believe it. When Jasper had called me three weeks ago letting me know about the opening for a position as a school nurse at Crescent High, I'd updated my resume and letter of application and submitted it.

With Austin being the principal and me dating his brother, he'd pulled the vice principal in to conduct the interviews instead, along with the current school nurse who was retiring.

Overall, I thought it had gone okay. A school position was seriously different to a shift in the ER. But I wanted it badly. Not only would it get me to the area and closer to Frankie and Ty, but I was excited at the idea of working on the sexual health program as well as the other general nursing responsibilities while working with teenagers.

It seemed like a fresh change of pace. Plus, not having to do shift work would be a fantastic win.

"Stop pacing."

I flicked narrowed eyes at Frankie. "I'm not pacing."

"Uh-huh. So just wearing a hole in the floor for shits and giggles?"

I huffed out a sigh and sat my ass down on the couch. "You know if Ty hears you saying that, he'll make a point of using it in every other sentence."

Frankie chuckled. "I know, but he's too distracted by whatever that garish new kids' show is on to hear my potty mouth at the moment."

I glanced over at Ty, who was snuggled in his little blanket fort we'd built earlier. Frankie was right. The kid's eyes wouldn't be leaving his iPad anytime soon.

"From what you told me about the interview, I'm sure you've nailed it."

My stomach cramped at his words. I'd said it went really well, but it was no guarantee I'd get the position. "I just want it so badly."

Frankie's gaze softened, and he clambered to sit, legs spread, knees on the couch to straddle my lap. "I want it too. And while I'm sure you did great, if this job doesn't happen, then there'll be something else."

I nodded, gripping his waist and tugging him toward me for a hug. I had no qualms about just how needy I was being, but the past four months together had been as amazing as they were challenging. I loved spending time with Frankie. Loved hanging out when it was just the three of us too. I may have had some extra love for the time we spent when he was buried balls deep inside me as well, but with Ty at the center of Frankie's world, I happily made the boy the center of mine as well. It meant time for sex wasn't always easy. But what it did mean was that it was usually hot and passionate, us clamoring for any chance to be together we could.

"Austin said they expected to make a decision tonight. He's involved with the post-interview conversation and has to approve the final hiring, so he'll let us know as soon as he's heard anything."

"Thank you," I said. "For finishing early from work to meet me after the interview." Frankie had been incredibly sweet. He'd picked up Tyler from prekindergarten early and picked me up from the interview armed with milkshakes and doughnuts. We'd then headed to the park and eaten them on a picnic blanket while Ty raced around the place, occasionally heading back for giant bites before zooming off again.

"Anytime," he answered. "I don't need much of an excuse to spend time with my two favorite people."

My grin stretched wide, and I tugged him closer. Our lips connected, feeling spectacularly right. "Mmm, you do offer the best of distractions," I murmured when he pulled away.

"It's a skill of mine. You got seriously lucky the day you met me, even more so when you begged me to pay you for a kiss." He laughed loudly. "Ouch."

I stilled my fingers from where they'd pinched at his waist. "That's not our story, remember?"

Frankie, still straddling me, tilted his face and reached up and smoothed his thumb over my brow before resting it on my cheek. "No. I was your hero, saving you with a life-changing kiss."

I chuckled, loving it when he was cheesy like this. But he also wasn't wrong. After that nightmare with Leroy, Frankie had stepped up big-time. Not only with that situation but the weeks following. In the end, there wasn't enough to take on a protection order. I'd been interviewed, but without enough to go on, it wasn't taken to the courts for petition. It had sucked.

But what had come from that was my friends stepped up. Jasper was at the center of it all. He'd done a round robin or something, spreading the word about what had gone on. It quickly came to light that Leroy had done this before with at least two other guys. I still wasn't quite sure how the group of friends, mainly Jasper's, were able to put a stop to his nonsense. But whatever they'd done, it worked.

I got a new number, a new phone, and security at work was aware of Leroy and had his details. But beyond the phone debacle, it was the last I'd heard from him. I did have a sneaky suspicion this man of mine may have had an additional quiet word with Billy. But I didn't push him on it. He'd tell me if I asked point-blank, and honestly, no one had ever done anything chivalrous for me before. That he had made my heart spring wide open.

"Hey, you guys decent?" Jasper appeared in the sitting area before we could respond.

"The point of asking but coming on in anyway?" Frankie asked, his brow arched. He remained in place, apparently having no intention of going anywhere.

"Please, there's no chance that nephew of ours is going to be unconscious yet. It's not even six."

I caught on the word "our" and angled a little just as Austin stepped into the room. My stomach clenched, and I swallowed hard, indicating Frankie to move. He did so immediately, though clasped my hand, giving it a firm squeeze. "Hey." I didn't realize how painful it could be to smile. But feeling like I could puke at any moment, the stretch of my lips felt unnatural.

I didn't want to ask, didn't want to start, and thank Christ Frankie was a pushy ass who said, "And? Did he get it?"

Austin looked at his brother and rolled his eyes. He'd worn that look of exasperation several times when focusing on Frankie. Austin concentrated on me and stepped forward. "Congratulations." He grinned.

"We'd love for you to start in the new school year if you're up for the challenge."

If Frankie didn't have a firm grip on my hand, it was likely my legs would have given way. Relief coursed through me, thick and fast, elation quickly following.

"Fuck yes!" Frankie hollered, wrapping his arms around me, squeezing me tightly, and planting kisses on every exposed inch of skin on my face. I exhaled loudly, the sound coming out shaky.

Finally, it was happening. I planted a firm kiss on Frankie's mouth.

"I'm so proud of you, baby."

"Thank you." I turned to face my two friends. Jasper could barely contain himself, his own excitement making him bob up and down. As soon as I detached myself from Frankie, Jasper was there, hugging me and congratulating me. Austin's hug followed.

"I can't thank you enough," I said, stepping away, my grin this time hurting for a whole other reason.

"I heard you interviewed excellently. Both said you were perfect for the job, and I know you absolutely will be."

I swallowed hard, emotion in my throat. "I appreciate it."

As if seeing my struggle, Jasper squeezed my forearm. "How about I crack open a bottle and you guys head on over to celebrate with a glass of bubbles?"

"That's great, thanks."

I turned back to Frankie. Pure delight was etched on his face, and it was all directed at me. "Move in with us."

My heart stuttered. I wanted that so badly. "What about Ty?"

"Ty," Frankie called. His son's head popped out of the fort. "Do you want Ian to move in with us?"

"Fuck yes!" He followed that with a head bob and disappeared behind the mountain of fabric.

My mouth fell open before my laughter burst out into a loud splutter. I clamped my hand over my mouth, unable to contain it any other way.

Frankie looked at the ceiling briefly, his lips pressed together. "I suppose I deserved that."

I snorted behind my hand, letting it fall away. My lips twitched when Frankie returned his gaze to me.

"But he's got the gist of it right. Fuck yes, we both want you to move in with us," he said, this time quietly as he hooked me close.

"In that case, it's a fuck yes for me too." I snickered before he captured my mouth, cutting off my thoughts and sealing our new start just the way this whole thing began.

With a perfectly epic kiss.

THANK YOU, READERS. YOU'RE THE REASON WHY IAN received his own story. It was your requests, your eagerness for more from him, that helped me bring his story to life. Be on the look out for Cody's story.

Want more feel-good romance? Check out my Outback Boys series, starting with *Stumble*.

And if you enjoyed this story, please consider letting your reader friends know, and I'd appreciate it so much if you could leave a review.

ACKNOWLEDGMENTS

A huge thanks to all of you who sent emails and messages requesting Ian's book, and then later voted for Ian's story next. I've loved (and am loving) writing this series. Kirkby is such an awesome town. Oh how I wish it were real!

This is definitely not the last of Kirkby.

As always, thanks to my publication team: Hot Tree Editing, Louisa, Claire at BookSmith, Donna, and Katie at GRR for the promo support.

My wonderful readers at RoMMance with Becca & Louisa receive an extra thank you. You guys are so supportive. I hope you know how much I appreciate you all.

ABOUT THE AUTHOR

I live and breathe all things book related. Usually with at least three books being read and two WiPs being written at the same time, life is merrily hectic. I tend to do nothing by halves, so I happily seek the craziness and busyness life offers.

Living on my small property in Queensland with my human family as well as my animal family of cows, chooks, and dogs, I really do appreciate the beauty of the world around me and am a believer that love truly is love.

To check for updates head to my website:
https://beccaseymour.com
You can sign up for my newsletter here and receive a free copy of *Always For You*:
https://landing.mailerlite.com/webforms/landing/r9f0i4
Plus, join my Facebook group, which I share with the awesome Louisa Masters here:
https://www.facebook.com/groups/rommancewithbeccalouisa/

facebook.com/beccaseymourauthor

twitter.com/beccaseymour_

instagram.com/authorbeccaseymour

bookbub.com/authors/becca-seymour